Trouble.

That was exactly what Brady Cameron represented to her. His charming smile and friendly nature, plus his obvious physical attributes, would be grist to the mill for her five built-in matchmakers. She could just see them revving into action.

How much attention would they pay to her protests that she didn't want or need a man in her life—especially a husband? Just as much as they had in the past: zippo.

Would she be able to stop their embarrassingly obvious maneuvers? *No.*

But if the situation escalated the way she assumed it would, could she confide in Brady Cameron and ask for his cooperation to avert their schemes? Maybe, if she was lucky.

But had she ever been lucky when she found herself opposing her five elderly friends?

Dear Reader,

Welcome to Silhouette. Experience the magic of the wonderful world where two people fall in love. Meet heroines who will make you cheer for their happiness, and heroes (be they the boy next door or a handsome, mysterious stranger) who will win your heart. Silhouette Romances reflect the magic of love—sweeping you away with books that will make you laugh and cry, heartwarming, poignant stories that will move you time and time again.

In the next few months, we're publishing romances by many of your all-time favorites, such as Diana Palmer, Brittany Young, Emilie Richards and Arlene James. Your response to these authors and other authors of Silhouette Romances has served as a touchstone for us, and we're pleased to bring you more books with Silhouette's distinctive medley of charm, wit and—above all—*romance*.

I hope you enjoy this book and the many stories to come. Experience the magic!

Sincerely,

Tara Hughes
Senior Editor
Silhouette Books

RITA RAINVILLE

Family Affair

Published by Silhouette Books New York

America's Publisher of Contemporary Romance

To all of my friends who have loved and supported me, especially Betty Teney and Betty Pollaci, who called me a writer long before I had the courage to claim the title.

SILHOUETTE BOOKS
300 E. 42nd St., New York, N.Y. 10017

ISBN: 0-373-08478-1

First Silhouette Books printing January 1987

America's Publisher of Contemporary Romance

Printed in the U.S.A.

Books by Rita Rainville

Silhouette Romance

Challenge the Devil #313
McCade's Woman #346
Lady Moonlight #370
Written on the Wind #400
The Perfect Touch #418
The Glorious Quest #448
Family Affair #478

RITA RAINVILLE

grew up reading truckloads of romances and replotting the endings of sad movies. She has always wanted to write the kind of romances she likes to read. She finds people endlessly interesting, and that appreciation is reflected in her writing. She is happily married and lives in California with her family.

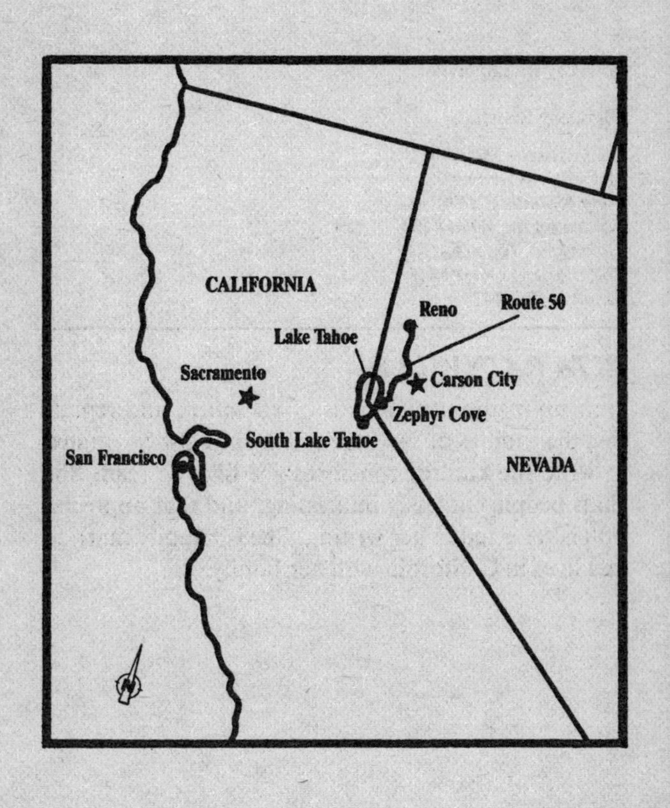
CALIFORNIA
Reno
Route 50
Lake Tahoe
Sacramento
Carson City
Zephyr Cove
South Lake Tahoe
San Francisco
NEVADA

Chapter One

"Well, I'll be double damned."

The stunned comment slipped out of Brady Cameron as he jerked his car to a stop at the side of the country road. His first glimpse of his new neighbor had jolted him. Justifiably so, some part of his brain informed him, because it was also his first glimpse of the woman he was going to marry.

His gaze swept from her casual hairstyle to her sneakers in a hasty survey as he withdrew his keys from the ignition. Dark red hair. Tall, slim, graceful. He couldn't make out the color of her eyes. They were scrutinizing the handful of letters she had withdrawn from the mailbox. After dropping the mail into a bright green tote bag, she reached back into the box and withdrew a sheaf of magazines and large manila envelopes. Satisfied that the outsized box was empty, she turned to walk up the curving driveway that led to the newly restored Victorian house.

Brady's gray eyes gleamed with satisfaction as he continued what had developed into a leisurely examination. She moved well. God, yes, she did . . . move . . . very well.

It was her concentration on the mail that prevented her from noting his car, he realized. That, of course, was definitely to his advantage, he decided, opening the car door and getting to his feet. It wasn't every day that he saw a woman who attracted—no, actually reached out and *demanded*—his immediate attention, and he was grateful that he didn't have to hide his fascination.

Now was just as good a time as any to introduce himself, he decided, craning his neck for one last look at her proud carriage and nicely rounded hips before she disappeared around the bend. He closed the door and loped up the road behind her. Two sharp lines appeared above the bridge of his straight nose as he frowned in quick concern. It was one thing to find a woman like this, another thing entirely to have her be available.

Within seconds, he had her in sight. She walked briskly, making the most of her long, slender legs. Although his eyes were riveted on the intriguing, utterly feminine rise and fall of her firm, softly rounded derriere, he was vaguely aware of movement in the thick tangle of brush and trees that lined the driveway.

So was she. After one sharp glance to the right, she broke into a dead run.

Brady's gaze followed hers. He narrowed his eyes, peering through the thick foliage. Yes, there *was* something. A brawny, lurching something. Definitely not the kind of thing that should be allowed to follow a path roughly parallel to that of the woman. His legs, moving like pistons, brought him closer to her.

"Veer to the left," he ordered softly, coming up behind her. "I'll go see who it is."

Startled, she glanced over her shoulder, breaking her stride.

Hazel, he noted with satisfaction, momentarily distracted. Brady liked hazel eyes. Somewhere, sometime, he had formed a theory that they usually came as part of a package deal with intelligence.

"No!" she gasped, swerving to the right and immediately disproving his theory.

"Damn it, stay away from there," he snapped, using his superior weight to nudge her toward the vast, springy lawn that circled the house. To their right, in the tangled brush, there was an ominous thrashing of breaking branches.

"See?" he added, trying to corral her and look over his shoulder at the same time.

"Leave me alone!" the woman panted, dropping the tote bag and breaking away from him. She managed to take exactly two steps before Brady's long arm wrapped around her waist, lifting her off her feet.

They fell on the grass, entwined, rolling to absorb the shock. An enraged screech tore through the air. Almost deafened, Brady partially lifted himself off the woman lying so quietly beneath him, and looked down at her.

No, that god-awful racket hadn't come from those softly curved lips. In fact, he decided, considering the circumstances, she didn't look a bit disturbed. There was no fear, no apprehension, no anger shading her features. If anything, her eyes held a humorous glint—and a look of expectation or anticipation. He tilted his head questioningly, his narrow-eyed gaze probing hers until her voice broke the spell.

"I *did* tell you to leave me alone," she reminded him, a thread of amusement warming her husky voice.

"So you did," he agreed vaguely, his answer a bit distracted because he was savoring the delicious warmth of her body, softly molded to his own from toes to chest. He was also enjoying the liquid quality of her voice. Shifting an inch or so to rest his weight on his forearms, he added, "But if I had, we wouldn't be in this very interesting, ah, predicament, would we? My name is Brady Cameron, by the way. I'm a neighbor of yours, and—"

The woman's hazel eyes shifted to a point somewhere beyond his shoulder. At the same time, Brady's muscular, six-foot-plus frame was half lifted, half dragged from her body. Stunned by the sheer strength of his assailant, Brady rolled to his feet in a defensive crouch and turned. His eyes widened, then blinked in disbelief.

Whatever he had expected to encounter, it wasn't two threatening, dark, beady eyes, a body covered with rusty hair practically standing on end, and a large, open mouth full of outsized, stained teeth. There was no doubt at all, he informed himself after a stunned instant: he was being glared at by a very large, very angry, orangutan.

"My...God." The words came slowly, matching his cautious examination of the shambling orange menace. Then, with a sigh he leaned back against a sapling and muttered, "I'm getting too old for this kind of stuff."

He cast a sharp glance down at the woman, wondering if she had the good sense to be alarmed. Obviously she hadn't. With a composure that he couldn't help envying, she rolled to one side, supporting her head on her bent arm. Once she was comfortable, she eyed Brady and his nemesis with interest.

"Hi, Brady Cameron. How near a neighbor are you?" The casual words were in direct contrast to the golden flecks of amusement sparkling in her eyes.

Brady's gaze returned to the ape, whose floor-length arms were swinging back and forth like great hairy pendulums. The twitching fingers looked as if they were rehearsing the finer points of strangulation. Shooting another glance at the recumbent woman, Brady felt his adrenaline reverse its fight-or-flight switch. It wasn't, he decided, that she ignored the glowering simian. On the contrary. She accepted it, took it for granted as much as she did the grass cushioning her lounging body.

Meeting her expectant look, he realized that she was waiting for an answer and he had forgotten the question.

"Neighbors," she prompted. "How close?"

"Next door," he said succinctly, wondering if the ape would leap for his throat at the sound of his voice.

He was spared that, but the temper tantrum that followed was almost as intimidating. The orangutan screeched, pounded the trunk of a nearby oak, then tore branches off the tree and threw them at Brady.

"Friend of yours?" Brady muttered, directing his question to the serene woman.

She nodded.

"He has a nasty temper," he informed her, dodging another flying branch.

"Jealousy makes him a bit irritable," she explained calmly, sitting up and wrapping her arms around her knees. "Normally, he's very sweet."

Brady confined his movement to his eyes. They shifted to the right and froze. His experience with exotic animals was limited, but in his opinion this one looked anything but sweet.

"You mean to say that this, this *thing*, is—"

She held up her hand to stop him. "Don't make him any madder than he already is," she advised. "But, to answer your question, yes, Zak thinks he's in love with me."

"Isn't that a little... *bizarre*?" he asked, trying to keep one eye on the woman before him and the other on the shuffling ape.

She nodded agreeably. "From our point of view. But he's been around humans most of his life and, lacking one of his own kind, I guess he picked me out for an adolescent crush. He'll get over it," she said with a grin. "By the way, we never did get through the introductions. I'm Sara Clayton."

Brady stepped forward, but a bloodcurdling screech stopped him. He retreated, scowling through another shower of leaves. "Do you think your friend will mind if I sit down?"

"Not as long as you keep your distance. Over there should be fine." Sara pointed to a spot about eight feet away.

Brady dropped down on the grass, disgusted.

Sara couldn't help smiling at his expression. Zak was a bad loser. He was an even worse winner. And right now, he was taking Brady's lower elevation as a sign of surrender. He strutted between the two of them, hands clasped over his head like a victorious prizefighter. He alternately blew kisses to Sara and directed a series of moist, Bronx cheers to Brady.

"That's enough, Zak," Sara commanded. "Go find Tabitha."

Zak halted his victory procession and stared at her.

"Go... find... Tabitha," Sara repeated.

After turning to Brady for one final raspberry, Zak awkwardly shuffled away.

"Is it too much to hope that Tabitha will offer him a banana laced with arsenic?" Brady inquired pleasantly, moving closer to Sara.

"Bite your tongue. Tabitha dotes on him."

Sara's examination of Brady was leisurely and candid. She watched him stretch out on the grass near her feet and reflected on the perversity of Mother Nature. As women aged, they dimmed and crumbled around the edges; men, however, seemed to grow more youthful and distinguished with the passage of time. Brady's years had to match or exceed her own forty-four, Sara estimated, but he moved with the loose-limbed grace of a much younger man. A liberal sprinkling of gray in his thick, dark hair and mustache accented his silvery eyes and deep tan. His jeans—not designer, she noted with approval—and short-sleeved navy sweatshirt covered a trim waist, flat stomach, broad chest and long, lean muscles. If he was an exercise buff, he was obviously the running-and-swimming kind rather than a dedicated weight lifter.

"Why did you run?"

The abrupt question broke in on Sara's contemplation of Brady's rough-hewn features. All in all, it was a nice face, she decided. She liked the laugh lines around his eyes. Also on the plus side were the creases in his cheeks and the faint dimple in his chin.

"Why were you running?" he repeated patiently, sounding as if he intended to stay put until he got an answer. "Were you afraid?"

"Of what?" she asked, startled.

"Of that." He pointed up the curving drive to where Zak was trudging along, grumbling, occasionally looking over his shoulder at the two of them.

Sara shook her head, her puzzled look fading to one of amusement. "Hardly. That was all part of the game."

Brady's brows slowly arched. "Game," he repeated, as if testing the word.

Sara nodded. "When I get the mail, he follows. We race back."

"Wouldn't it be easier just to send him for a swing in the trees?"

"Sure, but not as much fun. It's a harmless way to get some exercise. If Zak had his way, we'd collect the mail about six times a day."

"He likes to run?"

"He likes to win."

"I bet he cheats."

"So do I."

After Sara's grin faded, Brady reached back to see if his wallet was intact. Once that was established, he checked to make sure that the backside of his pants hadn't been torn off in the scuffle. Reassured, he sat up and faced Sara. "Who's Tabitha?"

"Zak's trainer."

"Does she live here?"

Sara nodded, then asked a question of her own. "Have you been out of town?"

Brady's smoky eyes rested thoughtfully on her expressive face. "Yes. Why?"

"For how long?"

"Several weeks."

"That explains it," she said with a pleased sigh.

"Not to me," he pointed out after an extended silence.

"Oh. Sorry." She plucked a blade of grass and examined it thoughtfully. "When you get home, you'll find an invitation in your mail."

"From you?" he asked, breaking in before she could continue.

She nodded.

"To what?"

"A party. Well, not really a party. More a get-acquainted barbecue."

"Great idea. When is it?"

"Last weekend."

"Oh."

"You see, when you have an orangutan in the family, moving into a new area isn't exactly easy. So we decided—"

"We?"

"My. . . extended family and I—"

"How many of you?"

"Six."

"Counting the orangutan?"

"*No*. Are you going to let me explain this or not?" she demanded, glaring at him in exasperation.

"I was just trying to help," he said, lacing his fingers around a bent knee.

"Well, don't. Believe it or not, I can manage." When he nodded amiably, she said, "Anyway, we decided to invite the entire town up to meet Zak and show them how well behaved he was."

"Were they convinced?" he asked in a neutral tone.

"Of course they were! Tabitha had him do some scenes from his movies—"

"What movies?"

"Haven't you been listening?" Sara asked with a frown. "Oh, I guess I hadn't reached that point yet. Zak's an animal movie star. He was in that takeoff they did of the Tarzan films, and then he did that biker series. Did you see them?"

Brady nodded reluctantly. He had indeed. They were brilliantly done and the animal's performance had amazed him. As a matter of fact, he had seen one movie three times.

"You mean," he said with a slow grin, pointing up the driveway, "that juvenile delinquent was the one who—"

Sara's laugh was warm and husky. "He's the one," she said proudly. "And Tabitha taught him everything he knows. She's had him since he was a baby."

Sara's hazel gaze met Brady's gray one. "When he isn't on location, this is his home. That's why it was important for the people around here to meet Zak on his own turf. We don't want anyone to be afraid of him."

"I take it you didn't make an appearance at the shindig," he said dryly.

"What do you mean?" she asked, puzzled.

"If he goes berserk every time a man gets near you," he said, pointing out the obvious, "either you weren't there or you kept a bag over his head."

"He was a perfect gentleman," she said stiffly, getting to her feet in one lithe movement. "And he's smart enough to know the difference between strangers politely shaking hands and a man who throws me down, rolls me on the grass and ends up lying on top of me."

"Smart fella," Brady commented, walking with her to where the tote bag had fallen on the ground. He picked up a few scattered letters and placed them in her outstretched hand. No wedding ring, he noted automatically, no impression where one had been, and no white band on her tanned finger. Things were looking up.

"So how did the party go?" he asked, picking up the last magazine.

"Just fine. Everyone joined his fan club. Want to add your name to the list?" she inquired with an amused smile, holding out the tote bag.

He shook his head. "Nope. In fact, I may picket his next meeting."

"You're going to get along with Emily, anyway," she muttered obscurely.

After a quick glance at her bland expression, he skipped the obvious question and asked, "So everyone in town was at the party except me?"

"Uh-hmm."

"Too bad I missed it."

"We all had a good time," she assured him.

"I'm sorry I didn't get to meet the rest of your family," he persisted.

"What a shame they're not home now," she said, obviously not regretting the fact at all. "I'd invite you up to meet them."

Brady stopped, looking down at her with a tenacious expression. "When you live outside the city, it's important to know the people living around you."

"I'm sure you're right," she said calmly.

"And I *am* your nearest neighbor," he reminded her.

"True," Sara murmured, stoically accepting what fate had dealt her. In the semirural area outside of Nevada's state capital, *of course* the only man who had good reason to be wary of Zak would be the one living closest to them.

"Exactly how close are you?" she asked curiously.

"As the crow flies?"

"As the feet walk or the car drives," she decided.

"A little over a mile by the main road."

"You say that as if there's another way to get to your place."

"There is. A path runs from your orchard to mine. About a half mile, I guess."

They reached the end of the driveway and stopped. Brady looked down at her with a wry smile. "Well, Sara Clayton, it's been nice. Sorry I can't say the same for your peculiar friend. But I hope that I'll see you again soon."

"Are you free for dinner tomorrow?" she asked abruptly, making a quick decision. "I'd like you to meet the family."

Brady didn't give her a chance to change her mind. "What time?"

"Come early, about six."

"Will King Kong let me in the door?"

"I'll meet you myself," she promised with a faint smile.

"I'll bring a change of clothes," he said philosophically. "Just in case he decides that shaking hands is too intimate."

Sara watched him fold his long legs and broad shoulders inside the car. She returned his wave, watching the car disappear down the narrow road. Turning back to the house, she muttered, "That man is going to be more trouble than a banana famine in Zak's hometown."

Not, she admitted fairly, that he had done anything to warrant that comment. Not yet. But the small-town broadcasting system had gone into overdrive the day of the barbecue. Quite early in the day, Mrs. Brixley, the plump owner of the Yarn Shoppe, informed Sara that her nearest neighbor was a widower, a photographer, and a charming man. Sara had immediately thought of an amiable octogenarian hobbling around taking pictures of trees. Before the thought had become more than a misty impression, Mrs. Brixley added that the models Brady Cameron photographed appeared on the covers of all of the famous fashion magazines.

That had drastically altered Sara's mental image. Mr. Cameron no longer doddered. And his lens became focused on shapely rather than gnarled limbs. She had restored a bit of his youth but had not dreamed of placing him near her own age. And never in her wildest dreams had she visualized him as he was in living and breathing technicolor—not truly handsome, she reflected slowly, just . . . *reeking* of masculinity.

Trouble. Innocent though he might be, that was exactly what Brady Cameron represented to her. His charming smile—yes, she would give him charm—and friendly nature, plus his obvious physical attributes, would be grist to the mill for her five built-in matchmakers. She could just see them revving into action.

How much attention would they pay to her protests that she didn't want or need a man in her life—especially a husband? Just as much as they had in the past: zippo.

Would they listen when she explained that one husband in her life had been one too many? Of course not.

Would she be able to stop their embarrassingly obvious maneuvers? No.

But, if the situation escalated the way she assumed it would, could she confide in Brady Cameron and ask for his cooperation to avert their schemes? Maybe, if she was lucky.

Had she ever been lucky when she found herself opposing her five elderly, lovable friends? Ha!

"Hi, darlin'."

The raspy voice startled Sara. She looked up, surprised to find that she had reached the end of the drive. Leaning against a fence post was a small, whipcord-thin, bandy-legged man whose face was all but hidden by a buff Stetson.

"Hi, Billy." She looked down at his tanned, work-roughened hands that seemed barely to move as they spun a rope back and forth, snaking out a lariat to drop neatly over a barrel. "Still practicing?"

He nodded. "Yep, darlin', 'cause someday I'm going to catch me a mischief-makin' son of a monkey with this here rope."

She peered under the shadowed brim of his hat. "What are you going to do with him when you catch him?"

"Ain't decided," he admitted in disgust. "Can't think of anything mean enough. But when I do, I'll get me one big, red monkey."

"What's he done now?" she asked with resignation.

"He snuck in my room and stole my new hat, that's what he done!"

"Billy! Not that gorgeous pearl-gray hat you bought last week?"

"That's the one," he stated grimly.

"How many does that make now?"

He twitched the rope off the barrel and rewound it. Within seconds he had another loop spinning at the end. "Lost count," he grunted.

"Did you tell Tabitha?"

He made a sound of disgust. "For all the good it did. Know what she had the gall to tell me?"

Sara shook her head, biting back a grin. This battle was not a new one. From the time of Zak's admission into the family almost eight years before, he had developed an obsession with Billy's western regalia. As soon as Billy purchased a new hat, Zak tried to make off with it. Billy now had a staggering array of locks on his doors and windows; unfortunately he frequently forgot to use them. "What did she say?" Sara asked belatedly.

Billy snorted. "She told me that them there orange son of a ...guns like to put things on their heads, and if I didn't leave my hats laying around, I wouldn't be coming up short all the time!"

Sara leaned back on the fence beside Billy, propping her foot on the bottom rail. "You ought to tell Tabitha to pay for the things Zak takes."

He ground the heel of his boot in the dirt. "Hell, darlin', I been doing that for ten years."

"Don't exaggerate," she said with a smile. "It hasn't even been eight."

"Feels like twenty," he grumbled. "Anyhow, she just says to put it on the bill. And she never pays me a red cent. The trouble is," he added, stating a gloomy fact of life, "she knows I got more money than I know what to do with."

"Billy," Sara said, her hazel eyes alight with amusement, "that's the saddest story I ever heard."

"Sara, darlin'," he said with a reluctant grin, "if I didn't know you for a real sincere type, I'd think you were being just a little bit sarcastic."

Her laughter spilling like liquid joy, Sara leaned over and gave the wiry man a big hug. "When are we going to have another lesson with that rope?" she asked.

"How long have I been trying to teach you how to do this?" he demanded.

Sara stared thoughtfully at the spiraling rope. "About ten years."

"Darlin', I hate to remind you, but that crazy monkey even learned how to do it. Why don't you just give up?"

Pushing herself away from the fence, Sara grinned conspiratorially at him. "That's why. I can't stand being outdone by a monkey."

"Tomorrow," Billy called after her, smiling. "Before dinner."

Waving in a gesture of agreement, Sara headed for the back porch. Before she could open the screen door, she was halted by a self-assured feminine voice.

"Sara, can you spare a moment?"

Turning, Sara fleetingly wondered for the millionth time how such a small woman could have trained and controlled so many large animals. As always, she gave herself the same answer. It had to be the Voice. It was deep, commanding, authoritative. It made her sound much larger than her slim four feet, eleven inches.

"Hi, Tabitha."

"Sara, you've got to do something about him."

"Who?" she asked blankly. Then, seeing the grim expression in the older woman's blue eyes, she guessed, "Billy?"

Tabitha nodded a "Who else?" nod. "Of course. Billy Bob Norton," she said grimly, "is on his bandwagon again."

"What's he done?"

Tabitha was almost speechless with indignation. Almost. "He had the audacity to send me a bill for another one of those overpriced, oversized hats."

Sara watched Tabitha impatiently push her short gray hair off her forehead. Her first impression of Tabitha, Sara remembered, had been that the older woman combed her hair, applied her lipstick and dressed in the dark. There had never, in all the intervening years, been reason to believe otherwise.

"I think the man's getting senile," Tabitha insisted, her resonant voice carrying across the yard to where Billy was standing. His rope skittered in a small, agitated circle. "Every time he misplaces one of those dreadful hats, he accuses Zak of taking it—and sends me a bill. Frankly, I think he eventually finds them and chucks them in the back of his closet. In fact, I wouldn't be surprised if that's *all* he has in his closet. It's probably the reason he wears the same disreputable jeans every day.

"The man is a nincompoop," Tabitha continued in a voice normally reserved for official pronouncements. "He has an aversion to apes, a monkey mania, a—" She ran out of words, casting a look of dislike at the man who prudently ignored her. "Look at him. He spends his days fiddling with that rope and plotting to get rid of an eight-year-old. By the way," she said, suddenly remembering, "Zak seemed upset when he found me. Did something happen when you got the mail?"

Sara related the sequence of events to an enthralled Tabitha.

"*Tackled* you? Rolled you on the *grass*? I thought you said the man was ancient. Sounds pretty fit to me." Tabitha stared suspiciously at Sara.

"Yes, he is," Sara acknowledged, keeping her expression bland. Tabitha was an unabashed romantic and regularly beat the bushes in hopes of finding a man for Sara.

"I was wrong. He's much younger than I expected him to be."

"How much younger?" Tabitha demanded.

"About my age," Sara reluctantly admitted. "Maybe a couple of years older."

"Really?" Tabitha didn't bother to conceal her delight.

"He's coming for dinner tomorrow," Sara said, wincing at the other woman's thoughtful expression.

"I think I better find Zak," Tabitha said, turning away with sudden energy. "We'll get to work on a special welcome for your young man!"

Chapter Two

The next day Sara kept herself very busy.

Hard work, she had learned—eleven years earlier, to be precise—was a perfect antidote for any one of a number of strong emotions. On that bright day in June, after fourteen years of marriage, when she had finally admitted to herself what everyone in town already knew—that her husband was just as unfaithful as he was charming—she had learned that particular lesson. It had been the same day she suggested that he pack his bags and depart, permanently. Remorse had clouded Roger's brown eyes for all of two seconds, then he had kissed her lightly on the lips and agreed that she was, as usual, sensible, reasonable and right.

It had taken him just a little over an hour to pack his tailored suits in his elegant luggage. All he left behind was their heartbroken thirteen-year-old daughter, Danita, a shattered wife, a large, rambling old house, and an even larger mortgage. After a swift divorce, Sara never saw Roger again.

Sara had decided at the time that the sages were correct when they muttered about experience being a good teacher. She learned, or decided, that charming men do not good fathers and husbands make. She never, ever, questioned that sweeping conclusion. The other lesson was the one about hard work. That one probably saved both her and Dani, her daughter, thousands of dollars in psychiatrist's fees. A third lesson—and that one came a little later—was that it was impossible to live a rich and normal life without friends.

With a lot of elbow grease and ingenuity, and a loan from an understanding banker, Sara turned her rambling home into a bed and breakfast. Her genuine desire to create a warm and gracious guest-home soon made it a paying proposition. The terrifying specter of a refinanced mortgage faded about the same time Sara regained her sense of equilibrium—and her sense of humor.

Her bed-and-breakfast setup underwent a similar transition. Within one year—her second as an independent businesswoman—Sara closed her house to tourists and welcomed five permanent, elderly residents. She'd had no intention of doing so; it just seemed to happen.

First came Billy Bob Norton, a frequent guest. He was an ex-cowboy from Oklahoma whose dilapidated ranch had apparently sprung a leak—of high-grade oil. His new prosperity, Billy complained, was keeping him "busier than a one-legged man at a three-legged race." Before the sound of his wistfully drawled

"Sara, darlin', in between these danged trips I need a place that I can call my own," had faded, he was entrenched in a suite of rooms on the third floor.

Next came Tabitha McGarry, an animal trainer. Using the Voice and what she apparently considered a beseeching expression, she marched Sara through several rooms on the main floor, waving her arms to verbally eliminate walls and conjure up a suite. It wasn't until she was settled that she mentioned the orangutan.

As if someone had posted a notice on the main road, the next three came within one week. Nicholas Carleton was the first to show up. A gracefully aging, urbane man, he explained that he was a consultant for companies that designed home security systems. Later, when he was comfortably ensconced on the second floor, Sara learned he was an ex-cat burglar who still regarded any locked door as a challenge. Even later, she found that he was drawn like a magnet to the supposedly impregnable homes of the landed rich.

"The police call that 'breaking and entering,'" she informed him, upon learning of one such escapade.

"No such thing," he returned coolly, glancing up over the edge of his newspaper. "I'm merely keeping my hand in. Besides," he added, "I don't take anything, so they never find out. It's just personal satisfaction. And sometimes I even adjust the wiring to improve their system."

Emily Pinfeather, Sara had thought in relief as she'd opened the door to the plump grandmotherly woman, would lend a peaceful note to what was already a melting pot of strong personalities. However, when a newscaster informed the local citizenry that chemicals were found in a nearby tributary and named the culprit, Sara learned that beneath Emily's ample bosom lurked the heart of a lion. Emily, in a word, was a crusader. She would chain herself to the gate of a nuclear energy site or storm a crooked politician's office at the drop of a picket sign. All she needed was a cause.

Arthur Marlow proved to be the quietest of them all. He was a retired stockbroker who subscribed to, and read every word of, the *Wall Street Journal*, *Forbes*, and dozens of other periodicals that even touched the fringes of the market. He emerged from his computer room every now and then to mutter cryptic comments. The tall, spare man with a shock of white hair eventually took over the portfolios of the four other elders and started one for Sara. He quietly disappeared every few months, apparently to shake the stock market by the scruff of its neck, and returned home with a benign expression and a bulging attaché case.

Once, when a meddlesome neighbor commented acidly on "Sara's geriatric ward," Sara became helpless with laughter. But that was the moment when she realized exactly how much these people had changed her life. She and Roger had been only children whose parents lived in the East. Dani now had five interesting, if unorthodox, honorary resident grandparents. And she, Sara, had someone older from whom she could seek advice. These energetic people had infused her life with enthusiasm and, in the process, become her extended family.

They also drove her absolutely crazy with exasperation. They had, each and every one of them, singly and collectively, decided that she needed a man in her life. Not a one-night-stand man; nothing less than a husband would do. And that was the reason she was kneeling in the flower bed removing the weeds that were mingling with the colorful patches of impatiens. She had already invaded the kitchen to bake four loaves of bread, waxed the gleaming dining-room floor, and washed her car. While she was so strenuously occupied, she didn't have the energy to worry.

Sara sat back on her heels and brushed a springy red curl off her forehead. Maybe Brady was just curious, she thought optimistically. Maybe he just wanted to meet his new neighbors, make a few welcoming noises, then return to his pretty models. She shook her head gloomily, remembering the gleam in his eye. She was not a conceited woman, but she knew appreciation when she saw it. And it had remained in his smoky eyes long after his lean body had been removed from hers.

Of course she didn't think for a minute that he meant anything by that sensual appraisal. It was probably a conditioned response when he was around women. God only knew she had seen a similar expression on Roger's face often enough—aimed at other women, of course. *She* could write it off as automatic male reaction, but Tabitha's response was another thing entirely. Tabitha would take one look at the gleam in his eyes and make one smooth leap from eligible-male-neighbor-of-suitable-age to wedding bells.

"Darlin', you still gonna meet me in the back?"

Sara glanced up, startled. After a quick look at her watch, she said, "Give me a half hour, Billy." Pulling off her gloves, she put them in the shed and ran to the house.

After a quick shower, she stood in the walk-in closet frowning at her clothes. After a moment's hesitation, she reached for a black, silky jumpsuit. "Vanity, Sara, vanity," she muttered with a wry grin. But she wasn't going to dress like someone's dowdy aunt—even knowing that Tabitha would take one quick look and allow her romantic fantasies to reach a new high. Running a brush through her hair took another minute. Some quick eye makeup, a few silver chains, earrings and medium-heeled black sandals added the finishing touches.

Sara was five minutes early when she walked down the stairs. Nicholas stood at the bottom, one arm resting on the newel post.

"Charming," he murmured, taking in everything from her strapped sandals to her flushed cheeks. "I understand we're meeting our neighbor tonight."

Sara looked down at the slim man who moved with the silent grace of a dancer. Rays of sunlight slanting through the long windows highlighted the silvery strands in his seal-brown hair. "That's right," she agreed calmly. "He had a close encounter with Zak yesterday, so we're going all out to make a good impression. Dinner's about six-thirty," she added as she reached the bottom of the stairs.

Brady slammed his car door and leaned against it, admiring the Queen Anne tower house before him. It had changed drastically since Sara had bought it six months earlier. It was similar to his, but cream and terra cotta, accented with dark brown and olive green, while his was done in warm shades of gold and tan.

The house had needed a good deal of work, and local craftsmen had been hired to restore it to its former glory. Much conjecture had taken place in the tavern as carpenters told of removing walls here and adding them there. As plans for the six individual suites had been revealed by the workers, popular consensus thought it a strange setup for a family. The details of those suites—in addition to those of the large kitchen, dining room, book-lined den, living room and screened porch—were the object of lengthy discussions each evening in the bar that served the town as a meeting place.

Brady grinned, remembering the puzzled comments as one final room had been constructed. A greenhouse, had been the unanimous opinion, as the large, wood-beamed glass room had taken shape. Heads had nodded complacently as banana trees in huge planters were installed along one wall. A variety of trees and plants soon adorned the others. Eyebrows had shot up and speculation run wild, however, the day a large, circular trampoline had been erected in the center of the room and long, cable-thick ropes were hung from the heavy wooden beams.

Brady started up the stairs to the wraparound porch when he heard an anguished, "*No*, darlin', do it *easy*," followed by Sara's laughter, coming from the rear of the house. Curiosity was stronger than politeness; he ignored the doorbell and followed the sound. With a half smile on his face, he rounded the corner—just in time for a loop of rope to whisper down over his shoulders and tighten around his biceps.

Sara groaned and closed her eyes.

Billy Bob held the rope taut with one hand and slowly pushed back the rim of his hat with the other. "Who the hell are you?"

Tabitha shot him a disgusted look. "Fool," she muttered, "can't tell the difference between a fence post and a—"

Zak interrupted her with a lusty burp.

Rushing forward, Tabitha ordered Brady, "Lean down and I'll get this thing off you." She shot a ferocious glare over her shoulder at Billy and said, "Let go, you old fool."

As soon as the rope loosened, Brady slipped it up to his shoulders and over his head. Tabitha fussily brushed minuscule bits of rope fibers from his navy blazer.

"Turn around," she ordered.

Amused at the tiny woman's brisk assumption of authority, he obeyed. "I'm Brady Cameron," he said when the small hands ceased their brushing.

"I figured," the small woman said with resignation. "You're early. We were going to meet you at the front door because Zak had a surprise for you."

"He gave it to me yesterday," Brady assured her with a straight face. He watched the older man coil the rope and toss it to Zak. As if he had been doing it all his life, the ape caught it and slung it over his shoulder.

"Howdy. I'm Billy Bob Norton."

The two men exchanged handshakes and measuring glances before Billy added, "And this here is Tabitha McGarry. She takes care of this sawed-off, cross-eyed, bowlegged—"

A dark, long-fingered hand attached to a long hairy arm lifted Billy's Stetson and stopped him in midsentence. Zak shambled away, tugging at the hat, settling it low over his eyes. Then he leaned against the fence and slowly unwound the rope. Within seconds, he had a large loop hovering over the ground.

Billy ran a hand through his sparse gray hair. "Tabby," he said in a muted roar, "I want my hat!"

"Zak," her firm voice commanded, "bring me the hat."

Brady watched as Zak curled his lips back in an ingratiating smile for his trainer, then directed a familiar-sounding raspberry to the older man.

"Zak!"

Sara touched Brady's arm. "This will go on forever. We might as well go inside and find the rest of the family."

Brady followed Sara through the back door, watching the sway of her slim hips. "Are the others as, uh...?" Realizing where his thoughtless words were taking him, he drew in a deep breath and searched for a tactful escape.

Sara's reply was succinct. "Yes." Indeed they were, she thought dryly.

But as the evening wore on, they weren't the ones who filled her with apprehension. Emotion crept over her as Brady's smoky-gray gaze lingered on her. It grew stronger as she realized his expression was one of anticipation. At least, that was what it was in the beginning. Sometime during dinner, it became blatant male desire. And he made no attempt to hide it. What was worse, her five companions grasped the situation at once. Their reactions ranged from suppressed excitement to quiet amusement.

"Emily," Sara said in desperation as Mrs. Mallory, the cook, moved flat-footedly around the table, serving salad, "I noticed all the letters you placed on the hall table for mailing. Is there a problem?"

"Terrorism," the older woman said placidly, spearing a piece of lettuce with her fork.

"In Carson City?" Brady asked in surprise. There was a wary expression on his face. Inside the plump woman with dyed brown hair and bland greenish eyes crouched a seasoned activist. She had already questioned his position on nuclear energy, feminine equality, seals and a myriad of other causes. His responses hadn't impressed her. If her expression was any indication of her feelings, he expected her to let loose with something resembling one of Zak's Bronx cheers.

"Terrorism is an international problem," she informed him in a patient tone. "We have to be ready to stamp it out wherever it occurs."

Sternly banishing a vision of her in fatigues and combat boots, Brady nodded attentively as she continued.

"You have to keep on top of these things or soon it will be just like the whales and puffins."

Brady arched his brows in silent inquiry.

"It's almost too late for them," she explained. "I could tell you stories of—"

"Know anything about computers, Brady?" Arthur Marlow neatly placed his fork on his salad plate. This was his first contribution to the dinner conversation.

Brady shook his head. "Sorry. Never used one."

"Pity." He scowled at the younger man. "Come in handy. Saved my neck more than once."

Brady watched as the white-haired man visibly groped for another topic of discussion.

Arthur brightened. "Have a portfolio?"

"Not for myself. I help my models with theirs, though."

"You can help others best from a position of strength," Arthur said obscurely.

"I suppose so," Brady agreed cautiously, wondering what on earth they were talking about. He hadn't decided how Arthur fit into the mixed lot of Sara's extended family. Billy, judging from the state of his clothes and conversation, was a down-on-his-luck cowboy who spent his time twirling ropes and looking for rodeos. There was no mystery about Tabitha; she packed Zak into her pickup and headed for Hollywood whenever they were summoned. Emily seemed to run around the country rabble-rousing. And Nicholas? He was also an enigma. The quiet man moved like Fred Astaire and had a subtle air of sophistication that was generally associated with money. Old money.

Sara's dark-brown lashes lowered over amused hazel eyes. If she were a proper hostess, she reminded herself, she would come to Brady's aid. Thank God she didn't worry about anything so deadly dull as propriety. People who did, she decided, missed a lot of fun. She would be willing to bet whatever Arthur had last added to *her* portfolio, that Brady was rarely so cautious or patient—or puzzled. She leaned back, prepared to enjoy their discussion.

"What I mean is—" Arthur warmed to his subject "—that everyone should have a portfolio."

Brady shrugged. "I'm not selling anything." Arthur's pained expression stopped him. What the *hell* were they talking about? The man's white hair was practically standing on end as he struggled for words.

"Selling?" Arthur's bug-eyed glare reminded Brady of an apoplectic editor with whom he frequently did business. "Everyone buys, everyone sells. A portfolio is as basic as breathing. Everyone needs one."

"Not in my business," Brady contradicted politely. "Only the sellers. And my pictures help them sell." It didn't take a towering intellect to realize that he had disturbed the other man, Brady thought, watching Arthur stab a piece of chicken with a ferocious thrust of his fork. Sara's amusement was all but palpable. It wasn't that he minded entertaining her, he decided after slanting a sharp glance at her entranced expression; he just wished he knew how he was doing it.

Arthur hunched a bony shoulder and muttered, "Pictures." The tone of that single word told Brady all he needed to know. Arthur had severed all communication with the nitwit who kept pictures in a portfolio.

Beneath the subdued clatter of dishes and cutlery, Nicholas leaned over and murmured, "He's a bear-and-bull man. Nothing goes into his portfolio unless it earns money."

Brady winced and closed his eyes for an instant. When they opened, his thoughtful gaze collided with Sara's, promising retribution and a host of other things. He forced his attention back to Nicholas, who was speaking quietly.

"My daily walk takes me by your house. Lovely place. It bears a striking resemblance to this one. Same builder?"

Brady nodded. "The same family owned both pieces of property."

"There's been a lot of activity around the house while you've been gone."

"I've had a contractor doing some remodeling and I wanted the bulk of it done before I got back."

"You're not altering the lines of that gorgeous place, are you?" Sara inquired.

He shook his head, a wry smile curving his lips. "And have the local historical society form a lynch mob? I wouldn't dare."

"Sounds like you've had a run-in with Mrs. Felton," Sara commented, remembering the intimidating president of the Historical Home Association. She had called the day she learned that Sara had purchased the Victorian house. She'd queried Sara about her plans for it and ended with a stern lecture about the legacy of old homes. One does not own history, she had stated; one is entrusted with it.

"Yes, we've had a few head-on collisions," Brady said. "We go a long way back. But I'm just making some minor changes, converting the back part of the house into a studio. Most of the work is done, thank God."

"I thought your work was based in Reno," Tabitha said.

"I've had a studio there for years, but I'm tired of commuting. It'll be a lot more convenient working from the house."

"Have you closed your place in town?"

"Not officially. I still have to get everything packed and shipped to the house." He frowned, thinking of the expensive, fragile equipment. "But before I can do that, the security people have to come out and wire the house."

Nicholas looked up, a gleam of interest warming his dark eyes. "Who's doing the work?" he asked casually.

Sara closed her eyes in supplication. Nicholas was in between jobs at the present time and his life was quiet. Too quiet. When Nicholas was bored, she remembered with trepidation, all sorts of problems arose. The last thing she needed, she thought with a mental sigh, was for him to start some of his cat-burglar shenanigans.

Nicholas nodded in approval when Brady told him the name of the firm. "They're good people," he said.

"As soon as the mess is cleared up, I'd like to have you over for dinner," Brady said, looking around the table, his eyes coming to rest on Sara's face.

"I'll be dropping in," Nicholas promised. With a small smile he turned to face Sara, his eyes gleaming with amusement at her appalled expression.

"Why don't we have dessert in the den?" Sara asked, rising hurriedly before Nicholas could utter further promises or threats. She glared as his smile widened, deepening the creases in his cheeks. Brady watched the exchange curiously.

"You go get comfortable," she told the others. "I'll bring the tray."

"Let me help you," Brady said quietly.

Sara's smile was distracted. "No, thanks. You join the others. I'll only be a minute." She turned and walked through the swinging door into the kitchen.

It was ridiculous to get upset about Nicholas and his proclivity for nocturnal, highly illegal enterprises, she told herself. He could take care of himself. After all, he had been around a lot longer than she had, and apparently his skills had kept him out of trouble.

For some reason, however, she failed to convince herself. He was getting on in years and he could have lost his touch. He could be injured. Or—God forbid—discovered. And if it happened in Brady Cameron's house, he could be in big trouble; because, beneath Brady's amiable exterior, she suspected, beat the heart of a very tough man. And that man, with the eyes of an artist and mouth of a mercenary, was nobody's fool.

"What's the matter, Sara?"

She looked up to find the cook eyeing her anxiously. Lois Mallory was about the same age as Emily and her appearance was just as deceptive. She was a wispy woman with the determination of a bulldog. Two weeks earlier, she had cornered Sara in the grocery store, pinning her against a pyramid of canned peaches as she declared that she, Sara, needed a cook and she, Lois, would accept the position. She had followed Sara out of the store, back to the house, approved the kitchen and claimed a nearby room for her bedroom. So far, the only one who had challenged her supremacy in the kitchen was Zak.

Sara dredged up a smile. "Nothing's wrong, Lois. I'm just thinking."

"You're going to get wrinkles, frowning like that. Have a piece of carrot cake. That'll fix you up."

Sara eyed it dubiously. "There's at least a thousand calories on that plate."

Lois quickly sliced six more pieces. "No such thing. Besides, you don't have to worry about that."

Sara stayed until the coffee was ready. When everything was on the tray, she backed out of the swinging door and crossed the hall to the dimly lit den.

Brady stood in front of the fireplace looking down at the blazing logs. He was alone. His jacket had been tossed on the back of the couch, the cuffs of his shirt rolled up to his forearms, and his hands rested on his hips. His silhouette, Sara thought, as her breath tangled in her throat, was a bold statement of masculinity. His attraction was potent, dangerous and not a bit subtle.

He turned with a smile, his eyes warm on her face. Panic beat in the pulse at her throat. No, she wouldn't let him do this to her. Once before when she had been old enough to know better, she had fallen for an easy smile and smooth words. The smile had proved to be meaningless, the words empty. Never again.

"Where is everyone?" Sara asked lightly, mentally heaping curses on the heads of her five absent friends.

Before he answered, Brady crossed the room and took the heavy tray. Placing it on a low table, he grinned and said, "Suffering from fatigue—apparently a highly contagious variety. First Tabitha yawned, then Billy. Arthur was giving portfolios one last shot when Emily poked him in the back. His yawn, right in the middle of a pitch for the stock market, wasn't as convincing as Emily's. Nicholas just shrugged and left."

He smiled again, enjoying her exasperated expression. Touching her warm cheek with his thumb, he said, "Don't get upset. I haven't enjoyed myself so much in years. Especially since they were doing exactly what I hoped they'd do."

Sara stared up at him in silence. She wasn't going to touch that with the proverbial ten-foot pole. "Sit down," she said finally with a sigh, gesturing to the dark-brown velvet sofa. "I think we'd better talk." Brady sat where she had indicated, tugging lightly at her hand and pulling her down beside him.

Sara wiggled her fingers, removing them from his grasp. "First of all," she began, deciding that honesty in this particular case was the only policy, "my five less-than-subtle friends decided some time ago that I needed a man."

Brady nodded. "I agree," he said promptly.

Sara held up her hand to halt his flow of words. "You don't get a vote," she informed him. "I've told them at least a thousand times that I'm not interested, that I don't want or need a man. But does that stop them?" She looked up to meet his fascinated gaze.

"No?" he guessed.

"Of course it doesn't. They drag home every available male they find. When I don't snap him up, they just go out and look for another one."

"*You* dragged this one home." His mild comment wasn't quite a challenge.

"Just to get it over with," she said. "I knew they'd pounce on you, and I decided to speed things up."

"How?" he asked lazily, watching her expressive face, letting his gaze linger on her tempting lower lip. He wondered if it tasted as sweet as it looked. He'd find out, he promised himself. Soon.

"Easy," she said, eyeing him warily, not trusting his suddenly bland expression. "We just spike their guns. I can tell them that I think you're nice, but you're just not my type; that I'm sure you'll be a good neighbor and friend, nothing more. Then, when the time seems appropriate, you can say more or less the same thing."

More unnerved than she cared to admit by his extended silence, she prodded, "What do you think?"

"I think we've got a problem."

Chapter Three

Problem?" Even as she asked, Sara was certain she wasn't going to like his answer.

"Not with the first part," he assured her. "I *do* think you're nice, Sara Clayton." His voice was deliberate as he continued. "Very nice. It's the rest that I have trouble with. Because you're exactly my type. And I intend to be a hell of a lot more to you than a good friend and neighbor."

He waited patiently, enjoying the rapid play of expressions on her face. Surprise escalated to astonishment, then segued into a rich blend of anger and outrage. If those few words had made her speechless, he thought wryly, how would she react when he informed her that he would soon have her in his bed? Watching her hazel eyes narrow, he decided that she wouldn't have a cup of hot coffee in her hand when he told her.

Sara took a deep breath. Well, she thought glumly, without a trace of satisfaction, she had been right. Brady Cameron was definitely going to complicate her life.

"You forgot the part about after spending years looking for a perfect woman, you finally found me," she said politely, her eyes a direct contrast to her cool tone.

He took a swallow of coffee and eyed her over the rim of the cup. "Not perfect," he disagreed coolly. "Just . . . right. For me. I was getting to that."

Sara's brows lifted in auburn arcs. "You mean there's more?"

He nodded, slowly dipping his head. "A few details."

"Why don't we just skip to the bottom line?" she suggested, leaning forward to replace her cup.

Brady gave a mental shrug. He'd meant to ease into it, but his lady obviously wasn't in the mood for tact and discretion. That was fine with him. The sooner it was said, the sooner Sara would be his. The sooner he would taste those tempting lips and warm himself in the fire glimmering behind her cool, hazel gaze.

Turning to face her, he said, "The bottom line is that I want you in my arms, my home and my bed—not necessarily in that order."

Well, he'd wondered how she'd react; now he knew. She laughed—at least her eyes did.

Her voice still one of polite inquiry, she said, "Do I have a deadline?"

"Before Christmas."

"How generous," she said lightly. "That's almost three months."

"It's two more than I like," he admitted. "Patience has never been one of my strong points, but if you have to do it the hard, slow way, I'll wait that long."

Sara blinked, watching his eyes darken with determination. "You're serious," she said, her smile fading. He didn't answer. He didn't have to. He simply looked at her, his face suddenly expressionless. Battling disbelief, she shook her head slowly and said, "You're really serious."

She watched as he placed his cup on the wooden tray and leaned back. He never took his eyes off her. Wondering how it was possible at her age to feel like a gawky adolescent, Sara yearned for a drink. It didn't have to be alcoholic, just anything in a glass. Cups had a tendency to rattle on a saucer, but glasses were marvelous security blankets when one's hands seemed twice their normal size and had nothing to do besides grow in one's lap. And, she thought distractedly, watching Brady's lips curve in a small smile, if a straw accompanied the glass, entire vistas were opened. A straw could be used to spear fruit and poke at ice cubes. It could stir drinks and occupy chunks of time by searching out the remnants of liquid in the bottom of a glass.

After an awkward interval, when the silence became oppressive, she burst out, "Is that all you're going to say?"

Brady took his time about answering. He shifted on the couch until his head rested on the back cushion, his legs were stretched out and his fingertips tucked into the front pockets of his slacks. "What else do you want to talk about? How long it'll take you to see things my way? What will happen when you do?" His lazy, slanted glance collided with her fulminating one.

"There's no sense in discussing something that will never happen," she said crisply.

"Then tell me how you and your... family came to this area. No, first tell me how you all ended up together."

Surprised at his amiable change of subject, Sara eyed his bland expression with suspicion. Then, remembering that a gift horse shouldn't be checked too closely and deciding that any topic was a decided improvement over the previous one, she nodded in acquiescence. But first, she reached for the coffeepot and looked at him with raised brows. At Brady's nod, she poured him a cup and one for herself, managing to add several more inches to the distance between them before she leaned back.

"Eleven years ago, my husband and I agreed to dissolve our marriage. He moved out. Dani, my daughter, and I remained in the house in Los Angeles. I didn't want to disrupt her life any more than it already had been. In order to keep her in the same neighborhood and school, I turned our large house into a bed and breakfast.

"Billy had been a frequent lodger and after several years he asked if he could live there on a permanent basis. He bragged about his new home to Tabitha, who had also stayed with us a number of times. She moved in shortly afterward. The other three followed hard on their heels. For a while, a very short while, I was a woman with a growing daughter and five permanent boarders. It wasn't long before we were a three-generation family."

Sara stared at the fire thoughtfully, remembering. She looked up, met Brady's intent gaze and gave herself a mental shake. Her voice was composed as she finished. "Dani grew up, went away to college, graduated and found a challenging job in Los Angeles. In the meantime, the city grew and swallowed up our quiet neighborhood. We all wanted to move; it was just a matter of finding the right place."

"It's a long jump from Los Angeles to Carson City. How did you happen to find this house?"

"Nicholas had a consulting job in the area. As soon as he spotted it, he knew it was what we had been looking for. We all came to see it and agreed."

It was Brady's turn to stare at the golden, crackling fire as he filled in the blank spots in Sara's story. Her cool voice and terse sentences as she spoke of her marriage revealed more than she knew about hurt and anger and a dozen other emotions she had carefully stored away. She asked for no sympathy, would have rejected it if it had been forthcoming. It hadn't been easy for her, he was certain of that. The conversion of her home to a bed and breakfast obviously had been the solution to financial problems, not just a whim.

"Wasn't it inconvenient to move from the city?"

"You mean because of work?" She shook her head. "My job is to keep the house running smoothly and Arthur uses the computer in his suite. The rest of them travel. Even Tabitha. Films are made all over these days."

"What about your daughter?"

Sara smiled. "There's a place here for Dani anytime she wants it."

"So you left nothing behind?"

"Nothing important. My life is here now."

"Aren't you ever lonely?"

Laughing gold-flecked eyes met curious gray ones. "You can't be serious. In this household?"

"What about a man?"

The smile left her face. In silence she stacked the cups on the tray. Brady gently brushed her hands aside and lifted it, following her into the empty kitchen. His question hung heavily in the air between them.

Sighing in exasperation, Sara turned to face him. One quick look at his expression convinced her that he would wait for an answer if it took all night. "That's a very personal question," she informed him evenly.

"I know."

Something about his voice reminded her of a dark-brown velvet glove—wrapped around an iron fist. "And it's absolutely none of your business," she said staunchly.

Brady extended his hand and touched her shining hair with a feather-light touch. "I made it my business when I saw you yesterday."

Annoyed, Sara glared up at him.

Two weeks later her annoyance still hadn't abated. Brady Cameron was slowly driving her nuts. It seemed as though every time she looked up, he was somewhere in the vicinity. If he wasn't out back with Billy, trying his hand at rope-twirling, he was listening with apparent fascination as Emily explained her thirteen-step solution to world hunger. He had long, intent conversations with Nicholas and even had Arthur mumbling in approval as he ventured an occasional comment on the state of the market.

Tabitha dropped down beside Sara on the porch swing. Looking over the railing at the velvety lawn, she said, "When I was in town today Mrs. Brixley was telling me about Brady's wife."

Sara leaned back with a sigh. "The jungle drums are at it again. I've been told by no less than seven people that Brady is eligible and ready to do some serious looking."

"His wife died about eight years ago."

"Uh-hmm."

"From all accounts, they had a wonderful marriage."

"Uh-hmm."

"People say that when he finds the right woman, he'll marry her so fast she won't know what hit her."

"I wish him luck. But it doesn't seem like he's looking very hard. There's one gorgeous woman after another driving past our house to his—sometimes several in a day."

Assuming her most innocent expression, Tabitha ventured, "Don't you ever wish—"

"No."

The word was quietly spoken, and coolly certain. Tabitha, however, could ignore a bomb exploding at her feet if she so chose. "Sara, you've let that man—"

"What man?" Sara asked lazily.

"Your husband."

"Ex-husband. Very ex."

"Whatever. By hauling around the bitter memories, you've given him a great deal of power. You've let him ruin your life."

"On the contrary. I learned several valuable lessons from Roger."

"Like what?" Tabitha asked suspiciously.

"Like how foolish I was to center my life around another person. How innocent I was to believe that merely by loving, I would be loved in return. The dangers of trusting a charming smile and honest-looking eyes. And that," she said in a tone of finality, "was just for starters."

"He couldn't have been that bad," Tabitha said with certainty.

"You wouldn't say that if you'd been married to him. You never even met him, did you?"

"No." After a moment, she admitted reluctantly, "Billy ran into him once. Said he was a ring-tailed bastard." That had been the most acceptable phrase in his highly original and colorful description. He'd also vowed that if it took every penny he had, he'd break the man if he ever came within spitting distance of Sara or Dani.

Sara smiled. "I rest my case."

Tabitha ruffled her short gray hair with an agitated hand. "Getting back to Brady Cameron," she persevered.

"Must we?"

"He's not like what's-his-face."

"You mean I can trust *his* charming smile and honest eyes?" Sara asked dryly.

"Exactly."

"But why would I want to? Tabitha, do you realize how peaceful my life is? How content I am? If I want to go somewhere, I go. If I want to do something, I do it. I don't have to explain myself to anyone or listen to complaints or objections."

Tabitha snorted. "A woman your age needs more pizzazz in her life, and Brady is just the one to supply it."

"I tried pizzazz once. I'll settle for peace, thank you."

"Well, you've got lots of that! A trip into Carson City is the high point of the week, unless you count the meeting of the Friends of the Library."

The ringing telephone interrupted what was obviously going to be a spirited commentary on the unremitting dullness of Sara's lifestyle. As she walked into the living room to answer it, Sara decided that whoever was calling, she appreciated the diversion.

She was wrong. The last person she wanted to talk to was Brady, especially when he sounded as if he was barely controlling his rage.

"Sara. Your ape just scared the living hell out of one of my models."

"Tabitha's ape," she said hastily. Ignoring his muttered reply, she called, "Tabitha! Come talk to Brady." After thrusting the telephone at the older woman, she dropped down in a chair and unashamedly eavesdropped.

"Hello, Brady," Tabitha said with pleasure. "What? How'd he get over there? Oh. He *what*? Well," she said weakly, "he does like water." Tabitha winced and held the phone several inches from her ear. "I'll leave right now," she promised. "Don't let him get away." Making a face at another explosion of sound, she cradled the receiver.

"Don't tell me," Sara begged in a failing voice. "Zak went visiting and Brady didn't appreciate it."

"Brady's model," Tabitha corrected. "Have you seen my purse?" She lifted a cushion and dropped it back in place.

"No. What does his model have to do with it?"

"Why can't I ever find that thing when I need it? The woman sounds like she watches too many horror films, if you ask me." Tabitha dropped to her knees and looked under the sofa.

Sara had read of people who claimed that their hair stood straight up in moments of great stress. Until that moment, she had believed it was a physical impossibility. Now, she repeated weakly, "Horror films?"

"Here it is," Tabitha said with satisfaction as she spotted her purse at the end of the coffee table. Digging for her keys, she said, "The twit had just finished the photo session and was in her dressing room. As she was changing her clothes—facing the mirror, of course; have you ever known a model who could pull a sweater over her head with her back to the mirror?—she said the door to the bathroom opened and this dark-gray hand with creepy long fingers and a hairy arm reached for her." Tabitha broke off to upend her large purse on the glass-topped table. "There they are," she muttered, grabbing the plain metal key ring.

Sara watched in fascination as her friend crammed the mountain of paraphernalia back in the leather bag. An orange and two bananas went in last. "What happened next?" she prodded.

"All hell broke loose. The model had hysterics and screamed like a banshee. She scared Zak and he screamed, terrifying her so much that she screamed even louder. By the time Brady got there, the model was on the dressing table and Zak had her sweater on his head. He was rummaging around looking for a towel."

"Towel?" Sara asked on a quivering note.

"Of course," Tabitha said matter-of-factly. "He was all wet from taking a shower."

"Tabitha."

Shrugging, she said, "Can I help it if he likes taking showers?" Her bark of laughter blended with Sara's infectious chuckle.

"I had the distinct impression that Brady was not amused," Sara said when they quieted down.

"Oh, God. You're right. I'd better go make my peace."

"At this point," Sara advised, "I think an abject apology will work better than explaining how fond Zak is of water."

Before Tabitha's shiny red pickup had traversed the curving length of driveway, the telephone rang a second time. Wondering if she would have to soothe Brady until Tabitha reached his house, Sara reached for the receiver.

"Hello."

"Sara, my dear," a firm, feminine voice said in relief, "I'm so glad you're home. I was afraid I might not reach you until it was too late."

Sara's brows rose in surprise. Mrs. Felton, president of the Historical Home Association was not a woman who indulged in idle chitchat. Her past calls, which Sara could count on the fingers of one hand, had all related to the modifications being made to the house.

"Too late for what, Mrs. Felton?"

"Oh, dear, please call me Helene, Sara. Mrs. Felton sounds far too formal."

Helene? When had they crossed the border of slightly guarded formality? she wondered. After a brief hesitation, she said, "All right, Helene, but you'll have to tell me what we're talking about. Too late for what?"

"Deadlines, Sara, deadlines. I've had the most marvelously innovative idea for our annual Holiday Home Tour but it will create an absolute avalanche of tiny tasks and I simply won't be able to do it without you. Please say I can count on your support!"

Sara stared at the vase full of colorful flowers on the coffee table. Was she being asked to buy tickets for the event or open her home to the ticket-buying public? It didn't really matter, she décided with a shrug. She had joined the association the day of the barbecue and intended to be an active member. "Whatever you need, Helene," she said without her customary caution, "I'll be delighted to do."

Several minutes later, Sara dropped into an apricot velvet chair. The woman was mad. She didn't want a favor; she wanted a bloody miracle! Looking around the room, with its gleaming oak floors and area rugs bordered in moss green, Sara was lulled by the serene beauty—for all of ten seconds. She had expected Helene to take advantage of her offer, to dump a myriad of nit-picking details into her lap. It wouldn't have surprised her at all; in fact, she would have been pleased. Sara loved old houses and furniture. She understood them. On the other hand, she knew absolutely nothing about writing a book.

"Not a big book," Helene had assured her, "just a tiny thing, a pamphlet of sorts. A history of the house. Naturally you would tell who built it—"

"Helene—"

"—and when it was built. And it would be nice if you could dredge up some peculiar family members. Tourists love reading about eccentric people."

"But, Helene—"

"Now don't be modest, Sara. I know you can do it. In fact, you gave me the idea the day of the barbecue. You told me that you always did the PTA newsletter for your daughter's schools."

"Nobody else would do it," Sara interjected desperately. "I never volunteered, I was stuck with the job!"

"Volunteer work is so enriching, isn't it, Sara? Just imagine—yesterday a mimeographed newsletter, tomorrow a bound book."

"You said a pam—"

"Besides, you have a new typewriter," Helene reminded her in a tone that declared ownership of such an instrument was the only qualification necessary for literary genius. "I'm sure that you'll do a wonderful job. Now the first thing to consider is research. You must *steep* yourself in the history of the house. Fortunately—"

"Helene—"

"—you have those records you found in the attic. Pull them down and start reading. Immediately. Two days should be enough time for that. Jot down a few notes and next week—just a minute, let me get my calendar—on . . . Tuesday, come have lunch with me. I'll have someone here who can help answer any questions you might have about the history of the house.''

And that had been that, Sara thought distractedly. The crazy woman had said a quick goodbye and severed the connection. Before she could give the subject the worry it deserved, Tabitha's pickup zoomed up the driveway, followed closely by Brady's silver Corvette.

About ten seconds later Brady was next to her, shouting. ''Sara, you have to do something about that overgrown monkey.''

''Ape,'' she corrected absently, staring up at the embodiment of male exasperation. ''Monkeys have tails.'' He didn't look like a man who had spent the morning working and rescuing hysterical women, she thought. From gleaming cordovan loafers, past soft close-fitting jeans to a tapered blue shirt, he was the picture of casual elegance. His rolled-up cuffs and open neck, revealing a liberal sprinkling of crisp dark hair on his arms and chest, added the final touch of wicked, male menace. Only his neatly cropped hair showed signs of agitation. It looked as if it had been repeatedly combed by his fingers. Come to think of it, she decided, taking a closer look, even his mustache looked a little ruffled.

''I don't care what he is,'' Brady informed her. ''I'm not wild about Zak when he's obnoxious, which is most of the time, and I like him even less when he pays friendly calls.'' Extending his hand to smooth a shining strand of hair off her forehead, he continued with less heat. ''Another episode like today and there won't be a model in the country who will come to my studio.''

"I'll talk to Tabitha," she promised, backing away from his disturbing touch. "She's the boss, you know. I'm only Zak's babysitter."

"She said she'd work with him."

"Well," Sara said more confidently than she felt, "then your worries should be over." One look at his slowly relaxing features convinced her that it was definitely not the time to discuss Zak's idiosyncrasies.

Brady's warm gaze slid over her face, stopping at the wary expression in her beautiful eyes. For the past two weeks, she had done her best to avoid being alone with him. And Sara's best, he acknowledged ruefully, had been pretty good. Each time he cornered her, anticipating some uninterrupted time with her, he had been shuffled off to twirl ropes with Billy or visit with the others. He had gone along with her machinations because it suited his purpose to do so. He now had five allies supporting his pursuit. But the sides were just about even, he decided, because the strength of opposition from one antagonistic orangutan and a stubborn woman was formidable.

"It's not going to work, Sara."

One quick look assured her that he was no longer talking about Zak. "I don't know what you mean," she said, opting for expediency rather than truth.

Wrapping his fingers around her wrist, Brady led her outside to the porch, where he sat in the old-fashioned wooden glider. Tugging gently on her wrist, he pulled her down beside him. He stared down at her mutinous face and said, "You put on your running shoes the day you met me. But it won't make any difference in the end. You can't run fast enough or far enough to get away from me, Sara."

Vastly annoyed, Sara tugged and withdrew her hand from his grasp. It didn't soothe her riled emotions a whit to acknowledge that she was free only because he allowed her to be. With a scowl, she said between her teeth, "Damn it, Brady, I'm not playing games. I've been honest with you. I told you right from the start that I'm not interested. If you're so anxious to find someone, why don't you come out from behind that camera lens and look at what you have in your house every day?"

Thinking of those who had stopped to ask her for directions, she added nastily, "Surely Bambi, Tami, Kati or Panzi would be delighted to help fill your lonely hours."

His gray eyes were coolly speculative as he took in her frown. Then he leaned back with an inward grin, wondering if she knew how pretty she was when she was mad as a wet hen. "Kids," he said succinctly. "Any one of them could be my daughter."

Touching her hair, then her earlobe, with a gentle finger, he held her in place as surely as if he had bound her with Billy's rope. "I want a woman, Sara," he told her in a voice as soft as silk. "I want you."

Sara blinked, trying to break the spell of his words. It took her a few seconds longer than she liked. He *wanted*. But just because he wanted, did it automatically follow that he had to *get*?

"You can't have me," she said with composure. "I'm not up for grabs."

His lazy glance slid over her still form. "You underestimate me, Sara," he said gently. "I never grab."

Sara caught the warning in the softly spoken words—and the determination. She rose and walked across the porch to lean against the railing. At this moment, she thought, more than anything, she needed space and distance. When Brady was near, she simply couldn't think clearly. And with a man this bullheaded, a clear head was essential.

Brady's gaze warmed with pleasure as he eyed her straight back. The day was unusually warm for early fall and Sara wore a sleeveless yellow-and-white striped blouse tucked into the waist of jonquil linen slacks. He was accustomed to pencil-slim women, but not attracted to them. There was nothing, he decided with intense appreciation, like the curve of a woman's small waist flaring to slim but nicely-rounded hips.

Sara turned, catching the gleam of satisfaction in his eyes. Irritating as it was, she was grateful. It helped to stiffen her resolve. "Go home, Brady," she told him seriously. "Leave me alone. There's nothing here for you."

"I'll wait."

"Damn it!" She wheeled away from the suddenly expressionless man, touching the handle of the screen door. "If you want to come visit the others, that's fine. But I'm going to be busy. Sometime after Christmas, I just may come up for air."

Brady stiffened. "Busy doing what?"

"Writing a book."

"A book?" he repeated blankly.

She nodded.

"The Great American Novel?"

"Don't be funny."

"Then what?"

"One about the history of this house and its occupants."

"What are your qualifications?" he asked with genuine interest.

"I have a typewriter," she said dryly.

"That's all it takes?"

With a rueful grin, she said, "Mrs. Felton thinks so."

"Don't tell me you're involved in one of her projects!"

Sara shrugged. "She volunteered me."

"Call her up and tell her someone stole your typewriter," he suggested.

"Does anyone say no to Mrs. Felton?"

"It's hard," he admitted. "The trick is to avoid her as much as possible."

"At least you agree that I'll be busy," she commented. He got to his feet and towered over her.

"Oh, yes, Sara darlin'," he said, mimicking Billy's drawl. "I think you're going to be busier than an ant at a Sunday picnic." He leaned down and dropped a hard, thorough kiss on her parted lips. "But I also think you're in over your head. I'll give you a couple of days."

"For what?" she asked suspiciously.

"To call and ask for my help."

Chapter Four

The following Tuesday Sara parked her Camaro outside the pristine white picket fence surrounding Helene Felton's two-story Victorian home. The house was classical Italianate. A square cupola sat on the low-pitched roof, which ended in widely overhanging eaves supported by decorative brackets. Windows on the second story were tall, narrow and arched, with elaborate crowns. Those on the main floor were rectangular with pediments that matched the one over the carved-oak double doors.

She pressed the doorbell, then tucked her notebook under her arm and waited.

"Sara! Do come in." Helene opened the door with a businesslike smile. Her silver hair was immaculately groomed in a smooth chignon, and her clear, soft skin made Sara think of a Southern belle who never ventured outside without a parasol. "Tell me about your progress,'' Helene commanded as she led the way to the parlor.

Sara's brows rose as Helene strode before her. The older woman's message came across loud and clear: no time was to be wasted on pleasantries. Her movements were as brisk as her voice. Those shapely feet in size-four shoes rapped out a businesslike message as they touched the floor and the ramrod posture eliminated any feminine sway of hips beneath the silk afternoon dress. Ah well, Sara thought, looking around, at least the surroundings were pleasant. Not exactly warm and cozy, she decided, eyeing the roomful of formally arranged furniture, but historically accurate and beautifully maintained.

''I'm sure that your book is going to be a tremendous success,'' Helene said in a soft voice, gesturing for Sara to be seated. ''Tell me all about it.''

''Pamphlet,'' Sara said gently.

''What?''

''You originally said a pamphlet. That sounds far less intimidating than a book.''

The older woman tilted her head and examined Sara with bright brown eyes. ''Nothing could intimidate you,'' she decided.

Somehow that statement made Sara feel about eight feet tall and correspondingly awkward. Memories of coping with a five-foot-eight frame at an early age, long before her friends of either sex had attained their growth, swept over her for an instant. Damning all diminutive women who with a few words could bring back old insecurities, Sara forced a smile.

''You'd be surprised how easy it is,'' she answered.

Helene raised her hand in a small movement, a gesture that plainly indicated precious time was being wasted. "About the book," she said firmly. "What have you learned?"

Sara sighed. "Not nearly enough."

"Why not? You've had five days."

Closing her eyes and vowing not to lose patience with the outrageous old woman, she said, "It's not the time, it's the lack of material."

"You told me that there were boxfuls in the attic."

"And so there were. But nothing goes back earlier than 1900 and the house was built in the 1880s."

"Oh." Helene was clearly taken aback, but rallied instantly. "It's a good thing I planned this meeting for today. My nephew is hopeless about many things, but he does have his uses."

Sara had the feeling that this brisk woman with the deceptively soft voice only tolerated people who had their "uses."

"Nephew?" she asked, wondering how many other people would be pulled in to work on the project. The small pamphlet, she thought grimly, was assuming alarming proportions.

"Yes, he'll be along soon."

"Is he a historian?"

Helene snorted, startling Sara with the inelegant sound. "Does a historian stuff vital records in cardboard boxes and hide them from his family? Or refuse to let anyone else look at them?" Her neatly arched brows drew together in a forbidding frown.

"It sounds a bit peculiar," Sara allowed cautiously, curious about the man who had buffaloed the indomitable old woman. More power to him, she decided after a moment. Helene Felton had obviously ridden roughshod over people for so long it was now an integral part of her makeup. It wouldn't hurt her a bit to be stopped in her tracks every now and then.

"It's not only peculiar," Helene said with more than a touch of asperity, "it's positively criminal. He is, of course, only related by marriage. My late husband's sister's son. He resembles his mother," she added thoughtfully. "A more stubborn man I've never met. He simply doesn't listen. He was like that as a boy," she went on in a vexed voice. "It didn't matter how many times you told him he couldn't do something, he kept at it until he proved he could. A most annoying boy."

Sara listened, thinking there was something familiar about the litany of characteristics being described. She grew more certain with each passing moment. But before the nagging thought could develop into certainty, a familiar deep voice, laced with humor, broke in.

"Bragging about the family again, Helene?" Ignoring her look of annoyance, Brady leaned down and planted a hearty kiss on his aunt's flushed cheek.

For the next few minutes, Brady annoyed the older woman until she was practically speechless. Every time she said more than three words, he interrupted, finishing her sentences however he wanted. Over the years, he had obviously learned how to beat her at her own game, Sara decided.

During lunch he switched his attention to her. "Helene told me that you need my help."

Sara scowled and would have given anything to tell him that he had misunderstood. Instead, she concentrated on her soup and gave a brief, cool "Yes."

"With what?" Brady slathered a roll with butter and tried not to grin at her escalating irritation.

"Everything," Helene said firmly. "If you have appointments for the next week or so, cancel them. Sara must have access to those records you have packed away if she is going to meet her deadline."

Sara looked up in horror and met his amused gaze. "You'll do no such thing," she stated. "We'll work around your spare time."

Ignoring Helene's brisk directives, he asked, "Exactly what do you need?"

"Data prior to 1900."

"That's no problem. I've got a lot of old stuff packed away."

Sara brightened. "May I borrow it?"

"No."

"No?"

"No. You may come over to my place and look at it."

"Why?" she asked baldly, barely hanging on to her temper.

"The book bindings are in poor condition and much of the paper is brittle," he explained in a smooth voice, replacing his wineglass on the table and eyeing it with satisfaction. "I don't move the stuff around any more than I have to. What else do you need?"

"Helene said you could help me with a section on restoration."

He nodded pleasantly. "I can."

Sara put down her spoon, eyeing his bland expression with suspicion. "What makes you such an expert in this field?"

"Didn't Helene tell you? Our houses—yours and mine—were built by one of my ancestors. Until about thirty years ago, when yours was sold, both places remained in the family. All of the old deeds, letters, journals and photos were kept by my uncle, in my house."

"And I can look at all of it?"

He nodded again. "At my house." His complacent expression was infuriating, Sara decided.

"When?" she asked between clenched teeth.

He smiled. "Any evening. Every evening. My time is yours, Sara darlin'."

Sara was still fuming an hour later when she drove home. The first person she saw was Nicholas, who rapidly received a blow-by-blow description of the meeting.

"Do you have any idea how long it'll take me to go through that stuff at his house?" she asked wrathfully as she turned to go upstairs to her room.

He shook his head.

"Days! Maybe a couple of weeks. And he'll be right there interfering and distracting me."

Nicholas watched, intrigued, as Sara turned away. Interesting. Sara, their cool, composed Sara, was changing before their eyes. Over the years, her patent disinterest in men had disturbed them all. Even he had been moved once or twice to alter his usual practice of noninterference, to bring home a few men for her to meet. He might as well have saved his time. But Brady, it seemed, was different. He had peeled away her insulation and Sara was as disconcerted and displeased as any other mortal who prematurely encountered destiny.

"Too bad we live in such a liberated world," he murmured before she had climbed more than a few steps. "There was a time when women had chaperons. I think the idea had something to do with the adage about an ounce of prevention and a pound of cure. It seemed to work."

Sara stopped as if she had run into a wall. Turning slowly, she stared down at him. He waited patiently, watching as her eyes grew blank with concentration. "Nicholas," she said finally, her lips curving in a satisfied smile, "you're a genius!"

The next day, Sara drove Tabitha's pickup up the curving driveway to the front of Brady's house. She removed the keys and tucked them in her bag.

Inside, Brady set the last box on the living-room floor. At the sound of a motor, he straightened and walked to the lace-curtained window. A certain tautness eased from the flesh around his eyes, from the set of his shoulders. She was here. She didn't want to be and if he knew his stubborn lady, she had spent hours trying to wiggle out of it, but she was here. Not, he acknowledged ruefully, entirely because of his charm. She was probably sitting out there telling herself that she would get what she needed in the shortest time possible and run back to her well-chaperoned sanctuary. That was her objective. But his was to keep her as long as possible and make the most of every moment she was with him. It sounded simple enough, he told himself as he headed for the door. But remembering the wary look in her eyes and the fact that she considered most men to be cut from the same cloth as her ex-husband, he knew he had one hell of a job on his hands.

His hand stilled on the knob. Sara had been running for years. Fortunately, he thought grimly, she had run long enough for him to enter the race, for him to be the one to catch her. He didn't know what kind of men she had dated since her divorce, but if her edginess around him was any indication, they had obviously let her get away with murder. It wasn't that he was interested in meek, bland women. Quite the contrary. And Sara, he thought with a sudden anticipatory grin, was definitely contrary. Thinking a little enviously, and rather fancifully for him, of early men who quelled their women with clubs and dragged them home by the hair, he opened the door.

"What are you doing in Tabitha's truck?" he asked, squinting in the reflected sunlight of the windshield. He leaned down, looking through the open window. "Something wrong with your—?" His gaze went beyond her and froze.

"Why do I have the feeling that you're about to tell me something I don't want to hear?" he asked, sweeping the shaggy animal beside Sara with a disgusted glance. "I don't suppose you just stopped to let me know you had to take him somewhere and you'd be right back?" he added hopefully.

"No such luck," she said cheerfully. "I'm babysitting. Tabitha's busy," she told him, mentally crossing her fingers. Giving him a moment to absorb the news, she added, "If you'd rather put this off until another time, I'll understand. The only problem is, Tabitha's schedule is going to be crazy for a while and I always stand in for her."

Sara produced a wistful expression, wondering if she would get away with it. She had never, she remembered, been very good at bluffing. What if he told her to come back later, alone? She'd never make that blasted deadline. "I really am anxious to dig into those books you have," she said longingly, "but it's okay if—"

In silence, Brady opened her door. Relief poured over Sara like a cool shower on a summer day. "He won't hurt a thing," she assured him as she slid from the high seat to the ground. "He's house-trained and he never touches things that are breakable."

Brady's eyes, which had never left her face, widened. "You mean he's coming in?"

"Well, of course." Her surprised tone matched her expression. "Did you think I'd hook him to a leash and leave him in the yard?" Looking up at him, she realized that he did. "I couldn't do that. He thinks he's one of the family. Besides, we learned a long time ago that his ability to escape ranks right up there with Houdini's."

Brady sighed. "Come on, Zak, move it." He watched as the ape slid behind the steering wheel, extended a long arm to the top of the door and levered himself to the edge of the seat. Waiting to close the door, he was caught off guard when Zak stretched up and planted a moist, noisy kiss on his cheek. Before he could react, the ape dropped to the ground, tugged at Sara's hand and shambled up the walk.

Sara bit back a smile and peeked over her shoulder at Brady. The look on his face was a comical blend of revulsion and astonishment. He slowly closed the truck door.

"Did you see what he did?" Brady demanded, coming up behind her at a quick pace.

Sara nodded. "That falls somewhere between a reluctant apology and a tentative offer of friendship," she explained. "Tabitha's been reading him the riot act."

Brady rubbed his cheek thoughtfully. "Tell Tabitha I'd appreciate it if she'd try explaining simple tolerance, without the affectionate demonstrations." He opened the door and gestured for Sara to enter.

"Oh, Brady, how lovely." The house combined the best features of two worlds. It retained the gleaming floors, solid construction and high ceilings of the Victorian era and added the modern touches of subtle colors and comfortable furniture. Taking a second, more thorough look around, Sara said, "This is the mirror image of my house."

"Right down to the grand staircase," he agreed, leading her to the foot of the stairs. "Have you discovered this yet?" His hand caressed the gleaming wood of the outer rail, stopping at the newel post topped by an elegant, glass-topped swirl. He slowly turned the ball and lifted it out to reveal a hollow core. "That was a hiding place for mortgage papers or the family jewels," he explained.

Reaching out to dip her finger in the exposed area, Sara said, "I should have realized what it was. We have the same beveled glass ball on ours, but I never gave it a thought."

Zak impatiently edged forward for a look, nudging Brady aside. He stood on the second step and stuck a long finger into the hollow space. Then, using his arms for leverage, he stretched up until he could see into it. Squinting horribly, he peered down the hole, first with one eye, then the other. Finally backing away, he watched intently as Brady replaced the glass cap.

"I have a feeling that he's going to dismantle ours as soon as we get home," Sara said.

"Let's go in here. I've already brought some of the stuff down," Brady said, indicating the living room. Sara followed him in, keeping one eye on Zak. Wondering if Brady realized how much his decor told about him, Sara looked around with interest. It was a room of books, good lighting, gracious, comfortable furniture and a few elegant antiques. He didn't require a house that shouted its masculinity, she thought. Taking a quick look at him, she decided that he supplied every bit of that particular quality that was needed.

Brady sat down cross-legged on the floor and motioned for Sara to join him. "We can start with this. When we have it in some sort of order, I'll bring down the rest."

Sara stared in consternation at the cluttered mess in the boxes. "There's tons of stuff in there," she protested. "This will take forever."

Brady nodded complacently. "I know."

"How much more is upstairs?"

"Lots."

With a groan, Sara reached for the nearest box. "Wouldn't it be easier if you just told me about your family?"

"Maybe. But that wouldn't help you." He dug into a box and drew out a handful of old photos.

"Why not?"

"Because you can't use secondhand information in your famous book. Everything will have to be documented." And because he wasn't a fool. He wouldn't impede her efforts, but he would be damned if he would hand her things on a silver platter.

"Oh." She craned her neck, looking around the boxes. "What are you doing with those pictures?"

"Separating them. Thank God someone had the sense to put dates on the backs."

"Good. I'll do these. Shove those boxes out of the way, would you?"

They worked in silence, dropping pictures on the rug in piles divided by decades.

"Which one is the 1890s?"

Brady tapped a pile near his foot.

Sara shifted to her hands and knees so she could reach the outer edges of the work area. Deciding that she could examine the pictures at length once they were separated, she turned them over and swiftly dealt them into the proper stacks. After a few minutes, she slowed down and looked over her shoulder. Brady was leaning back against the couch with a pleasantly intrigued expression on his face. His eyes swept over her sweater to her jean-clad legs and back again, lingering on her firm, softly rounded derriere.

A tingle of awareness shot through her as his smoky-gray eyes captured hers. She had a fleeting impression of a silvery-eyed, primitive man closing in on the woman of his choice. Drawing a ragged breath, Sara wondered how she could ever, even for an instant, have relegated him to a "safe" category. Frightening in his intensity at this instant, Brady was not son, nephew or neighbor. What he was, was *male*. He didn't move, but Sara slowly leaned back on her heels, resisting his silent command.

"No, Brady."

His mustache curved with his small smile. "No, what?"

"Whatever you're asking," she said, rattled.

"Actually," he said, extending his hand to her, "what I'm doing is inviting."

Sara shook her head slowly back and forth.

"Come here, sweetheart."

Sara tucked her hands between her thighs and narrowed her eyes. His voice, husky with desire, settled over her like a warm cloak.

"Give me your hand, Sara."

She tightened her thighs, fighting the impulse to reach out and lace her fingers with his. His tanned hands were warm and strong . . . and inviting.

"Sara?"

"This is ridiculous!" she burst out, feeling a rush of heat course through her body. She couldn't remember when she had last felt so awkward—or tempted. Groping frantically for her friendly-neighbor or let's-be-pals speech, she looked directly at him. That was a mistake. His gaze had never left her. He was waiting, patiently, as if he had all the time in the world.

Unnerved, she said in a reasonable tone, "Brady, can't we just be friends? Isn't that enough?"

"No." He moved his fingers, silently urging her hand to his. "I have a lot of friends and frankly, Sara, that's not at all what I have in mind for you." His voice lowered another notch. "Take my hand, honey."

"Brady, this is foolish," she complained, slowly releasing her hand and lifting it to his. "This isn't going to prove a thing."

His fingers closed over hers. "It proves that you trust me."

"No, it doesn't," she protested, resisting the steady pressure that would eventually pull her right into his arms. "It just means that I'm feeling a little embarrassed and a lot foolish, and it seems the easiest way to end this little contretemps."

His mustache twitched when he grinned. "Honey, hasn't anyone warned you about the dangers of following the easy path?"

"Look," she said desperately, as her traitorous body followed her hand, "you must know that you're very attractive—"

"Thank you," he murmured as she slid into his arms. "So are you."

"Brady!" she exclaimed, as his lips closed in on hers. "That's not what I meant, and you know—"

As a kiss, she decided hazily, it was fairly shattering. His lips were just like his hands—warm and strong. Everything about the man was warm and strong...and tempting.

She opened her eyes and looked up into a silvery gaze gleaming with masculine satisfaction. Clearing her throat, she said, "I'm going to wrinkle the pictures."

"No, you won't," he murmured, touching the corner of her mouth in a whisper of a kiss.

"They're fragile," she reminded him breathlessly.

"Don't move. They'll be just fine." His forearms rested by her shoulders, effectively imprisoning her against the floor.

"What I meant before—" She stopped as his lips rested on the frantic pulse beating in the hollow of her throat.

"Hmm?"

"—was that I—" She moved her head restlessly as his lips moved to the tender juncture of her throat and shoulder.

"Hmm?"

"—don't trust attractive men."

He pressed one last hard kiss on her parted lips before he shifted his position, lifting his chest from the soft cushion of her breasts and resting his weight on his arms. Looking down at her, he said, "You don't trust any man. But you will, Sara. You will."

He reluctantly eased himself away, stood up and leaned over to take Sara's hand. Pulling her to her feet, he said, "I just realized that King Kong hasn't tried to dismember me. What do you suppose he's up to?"

It took Sara a moment to switch gears. She was still adjusting to the loss of his body heat, missing it, even as her sorely-tried defence mechanism seemed to sigh in relief. "What?"

"Zak," he repeated.

"Probably exploring," she said vaguely. "Maybe we'd better go look."

"We don't have to worry about my studio. It's locked."

"Thank God for that. He's fascinated by mechanical things. He'd probably be in there unscrewing all your lenses. You didn't leave any keys lying around, did you?"

"Why? Is he also a part-time burglar?"

She winced, thinking of the hours Nicholas spent with Zak, teaching him the finer art of breaking and entering. "He just likes to fiddle with locks and keys," she said evasively.

Brady laced his fingers through hers. "Come on, let's chase him down."

They wound their way through the main floor, stopping at the stairway.

"I hate to mention this," Sara said, "but do you hear water running?"

Brady's oath was succinct and explicit.

They tore up the stairs, instinctively turning to the master bedroom.

"This way," Brady said, tugging at her hand. He led her through the room, not slowing down until he reached the bath. Sara was vaguely aware of a lot of dark brown lightened by touches of gold and a splash of orange.

They came to a halt at the bathroom door. Zak was stretched out in a huge, glass-encased, circular marble sunken tub, a look of bliss on his face. Several different shower heads directed a fine spray at him. Raising his eyes from contemplating the drops of water hitting his belly, he waved a laconic hand.

"My God."

"You can say that again," Sara said dryly, looking around the spacious room. Wordlessly she examined the luxuriant ferns, the overhead heat lamps, the stained-glass skylight and, of course, the tub.

Brady grimaced, easily reading her expressive face. He had once again been cast in the role of a playboy who conducted orgies and God only knew what else in this sybaritic room.

"Any idea how we get him out of there?" he asked grimly.

Sara frowned. "Unless you have a way of shutting the water off out here, I go in and get him."

He watched as Zak curled his lips in an ingratiating smile. "I'll do it."

She shook her head. "My ape, my problem."

"What would happen if we just leave him there?"

"Your water bill would never be the same. He'd stay there for hours." Gesturing to the thick carpeting, she said, "If you'll have some towels ready, I think that'll come out unscathed." Kicking off her shoes, she reached for the shower door.

Her clothes were plastered to her before she had a chance to close it behind her. Zak shook his head and stretched out his long arms to stop her from turning off the water, but since he wouldn't use the strength in his powerful hands against her, it was a simple matter for Sara to turn the handles. She leaned over to maintain eye contact with the cranky ape and sighed when he turned his face away.

It didn't help that Brady was watching every move she made. She could feel his eyes on her—and on the saturated clothes that faithfully clung to every curve and hollow of her body.

She touched Zak gently on the shoulder and waited for him to look at her. When he did, using the sign language that Tabitha had taught them both, she signaled that they had to go. Zak pursed his mobile lips and blew a disgusted raspberry.

Brady opened the door, handed her a towel and spread one on the rug.

"Thanks." Sara briskly rubbed Zak down, then tossed him the towel and said, "You can finish the job." He dropped to the floor and meticulously ran the edge of the towel between his toes.

She took another towel from Brady and began working on her hair. She felt it as soon as he left the room. Only seconds later, her fine-edged awareness returned and she knew he was back.

"Here." Brady handed her a maroon velvet robe. "I hate to sound like something out of an old movie, but you can't walk around like that. I'll take Zak downstairs while you change. Bring your things down and put them in the dryer."

"Brady?" He turned, brows raised, a challenge in his silence. The polite words she had ready died in her throat. "It's easier for Zak to walk erect if you let him hold your hand."

Relieved that she didn't argue, he nodded. He wasn't about to leave an infatuated, too-human ape with her while she removed her clothes. Holding out his hand to Zak, he said, "C'mon, pest, I'll see if I can rustle you up a banana." He closed the door and drew in a deep breath. Moving away from Sara had been hard enough downstairs. And now, with her jeans and sweater looking as if they were painted on, it took all his resolution to keep on walking. But he wasn't going to blow it now. He wanted her to come back. Hell, he wanted her, period.

Looking down at Zak, he muttered, "And you can bet your last banana that I'm going to get her."

Chapter Five

Brady unlocked the front door and came to a halt on the threshold. A dim light shone at the end of the hall that led to the family room. Earlier in the evening, when he'd left, the house had been dark. He had never believed that an illuminated room would discourage or deter a burglar with an IQ higher than thirteen. Nor did he leave lights on to create the illusion that someone was waiting for him. But when Sara moved in, there would be lights gleaming in the windows and he damned well wouldn't have to turn them on for himself.

If he was sensible, he told himself, he'd back right out, get to the nearest telephone and call the police. But considering the low crime rate in the valley, that he had no known enemies, and that only a cretin would break in, turn on a light, and wait for trouble, it seemed unreasonable to panic. Besides, prudence had never been his strong point.

Thinking that sensible people must lead extraordinarily dull lives, he closed the door. Avoiding the floorboards that creaked, he quietly traversed the length of the hall—and stopped, taking in the homey scene before him.

Nicholas calmly glanced up from the newspaper he was reading. A glass of Brady's most expensive brandy was near his elbow. "I expected you long before this," he said cordially.

Brady's dark brows rose in surprise. "Sorry," he said dryly, "I got held up. I would have moved things along if I'd known I had company." Looking around, he asked, "Are you alone?"

The older man's voice was calm as he neatly folded the paper and placed it on the table beside him. "Sara isn't here, if that's what you mean."

Brady nodded his head in acknowledgment. That was exactly what he'd meant. "And why are *you* here, Nicholas?" he asked coolly. "Not that you aren't welcome, of course. I just don't remember setting up an appointment."

Nicholas's lips curved in a wry smile. "Or inviting me?"

Brady nodded again. "That too. Although that first night I had dinner at your place, I did mention having you all over. It seems I've moved too slowly."

"Not at all," Nicholas assured him politely.

Brady indicated the glass of brandy. "Is there any of that left?"

"Of course. The decanter's almost full."

Brady splashed some of the potent liquid into a glass and sat down. Lifting the glass in a silent toast, he took a swallow. Nicholas was apparently in no hurry to speak so he leaned back and eyed him speculatively. Had the older man taken one of his walks and merely dropped in for a visit? If that was the case, why hadn't he been repelled by the fancy and exorbitantly priced new alarm system? He decided that whatever reason Nicholas had for visiting, the same question remained: how the hell had he gotten inside the house?

He was about to ask, when another question stopped him. Had Nicholas been elected by the others to represent the family? Was he there—Brady's mustache twitched at the thought—in place of Sara's father, to inquire what his intentions were toward her? It wouldn't be an unreasonable act for a man of his age and generation. But if he was, the situation didn't seem to bother him. He was serenely gazing at the sparking fire in the hearth.

"I'm going to marry her," Brady said abruptly, deciding to remove the burden from Nicholas's shoulders. "I love her. It would be nice if you all approve; but even if you don't, with or without your help, I'm going to marry her."

"Sara?" Nicholas inquired mildly.

Brady stared at him, perplexed. "Of course, Sara. Isn't that why you're here?"

"No."

"No?"

"No."

"Oh."

"But since you assume I have the right to be heard, I will say one thing. I didn't meet Sara until two years after her divorce. She was still painfully and gallantly piecing her life back together.'' His face was expressionless as he watched the younger man. ''I never want to see her that way again. You'll answer to me if you hurt her.''

Brady got a quick glimpse of the man behind the urbane facade. A man whose strength was not diminished by his slim frame or advanced age. A man who had few emotional ties and who would zealously guard those he had.

''I won't hurt her,'' Brady said quietly.

Nicholas eyed him steadily, then without moving a muscle seemed to relax.

Brady waited. After several beats of silence he said, ''Nicholas, what are you doing in my house, reading my paper and drinking my best brandy? And what's more to the point, how did you get in?'' He watched as the slim man smiled and settled more comfortably in his chair.

''I told you I'd be dropping by.''

''So you did, but I thought you meant in a more conventional way.''

''I rarely do the expected. That's one of my charms.'' His eyes narrowed in amusement. ''Has Sara never mentioned my line of work?''

Brady shook his head, watching the other man intently. Nicholas was obviously enjoying himself.

''I'm a consultant,'' he explained. ''With...a rather extensive background of practical experience.''

''Who do you work for?'' Brady asked. His eyebrows shot up when Nicholas mentioned the name of the company. "I've heard of them. They have a good reputation."

"They're the best," Nicholas said simply.

Content to let the older man come to the point in his own good time, Brady asked lazily, "And exactly what kind of consulting do you do for them?"

"I think you could call me a troubleshooter. I look for flaws, bugs, glitches—whatever name they go by these days."

"You inspect the plans?"

"No, I work at the site."

"Ah. You do a final inspection?"

"In a manner of speaking."

"All right, Nicholas, I'll bite. How do you do it?"

"The same way I got in here. I break in."

Brady's glass clinked on the table as he brought it down with more force than necessary. "Break in?" he repeated.

"Uh-hmm."

"You go around breaking into houses? That's your job?"

Nicholas nodded.

"And tonight? My house?"

Nicholas moved his hand in an airy gesture. "A neighborly token of friendship. And," he admitted slowly, "a bit of a busman's holiday. Things have been quiet lately."

"You're running out of work?" Brady asked politely, still trying to reconcile the aristocratic old man and his chosen profession.

"That's one of the hazards," Nicholas said with a shrug. "Every time I pinpoint a weak spot, they improve the system. It's getting tougher all the time."

"Why do you do it?"

Nicholas grinned, giving Brady a second glimpse of another, younger man. "The challenge. Unless you work at it, life gets pretty dull after you turn sixty." Pulling a folded paper out of his shirt pocket, he said, "Before I forget, give this to the people who did your work. Landis, isn't it?" At Brady's nod, he added, "They'll know what to do."

"And what'll I tell them when they ask how I know?"

"Tell them you had it checked by a pro," Nicholas said with a chuckle.

Brady looked at him curiously. "What did you do before you joined forces with the company?"

"Much the same."

"On which side of the law?" he asked with interest.

"I was known by my peers as a modern Robin Hood," Nicholas said with a reminiscent smile.

Brady eyed him with fascination. "Does Sara know?"

Nicholas nodded. "It was a bit of a shock, but she's resilient."

"How does she feel about it?"

"Distinctly edgy. Didn't you notice how nervous she got the night I mentioned dropping in on you? I think she's afraid I'll lose my touch and end up in the pokey."

"Have you ever done time?"

Nicholas raised an eyebrow at the blunt question, then shook his head. "Most of my...clients weren't in a position to complain to the police." In answer to Brady's mute inquiry, he explained. "If a man bought a stolen painting and added it to his own private collection, he could hardly report the theft when he came home one evening and found it missing."

Impressed despite himself, Brady said, "Sounds like you worked in the big league."

"I did."

"It also sounds like it could be dangerous."

"It was. But quite satisfying. And never, never dull," Nicholas uncrossed his legs and stood up, his movements lithe and graceful. "This has been an enjoyable evening. I'll drop in again sometime."

"Through the front door?" Brady asked with a hint of a smile.

"Not if there's a more interesting way to do it."

As the two men walked to the door, Nicholas asked, "Does Sara know that you intend to marry her?"

"No. She seems to think that I'm just after a hot, quick affair."

"I wonder how she got that impression," Nicholas murmured, gazing at the younger man.

"Beats me," Brady said with a shrug.

"Why don't you tell her?"

"Because the thought of marriage scares the living daylights out of her, and I don't want her running any faster than she is already."

Brady bounded up the stairs to the porch, gave a token knock on Sara's front door, then reached for the knob. Before he could turn it, the door swung open. Zak, decked out in a hotel doorman's gold-braided cap that rested precariously just above his eyes, stood rigidly at attention, his knuckles resting on the floor.

Recognizing both the hat and demeanor from one of Zak's early films, Brady groaned.

"Where's Sara?" he demanded, then stopped, a spasm crossing his face. My God, they had him doing it. "Forget it," he commanded. Just as he was about to turn away, Zak nodded and curled back his lips in a wide, amiable grin. The movement shifted the hat over his eyes and he raised a long arm to adjust it.

By the time he had accomplished that feat, Brady stood in the doorway to the living room. He stopped, drinking in the sight of Sara curled up on a forest-green velvet couch. The dark fire of her hair gleamed in the shifting rays of the early afternoon sunlight.

Sara looked up from her book, astonished by the sudden leap of her senses. Every one of them came alive at the very sight of him. *Nobody* should have that effect on a sensible, rational person, she thought darkly. And normally no one did—assuming that she was the sensible, rational person in question. But Brady Cameron was definitely an exception to the rule. If she wanted to continue living peacefully in this gracious old house that she had loved at first sight, she thought, she had to do something about it. And she would, she decided stoutly. As soon as she figured out precisely what that something should be.

A shiver ran through her as he stood in the doorway, just looking. And, damn his smoky eyes, he knew it! Sitting up and making a show of rubbing her arms briskly, she said casually, "Hi, Brady. It's turning a little cool, isn't it?"

He thoughtfully considered the sunlight pouring through the windows, then turned back to her. "For October, in this neck of the woods, it's quite warm," he said blandly. The look in his eyes informed her that she'd have to do better than that.

Brady strolled into the room and sat beside her. "What are you reading?" he asked, touching the book that rested in her lap. She turned it over and showed him the title.

"It's one of the journals from this branch of your family tree. One that I found in the attic." Smiling, she added, "I must say, you had some pretty peculiar relatives. There was one old geezer who used this place as a winter residence, much to the annoyance of the lady of the house. Every spring, he'd take a packhorse and disappear into the mountains to dig for silver. Every winter, he'd be back with rheumatism and a bundle of filthy laundry."

"No silver?"

"Not an ounce. At least, not so far."

"Let's take a peek at the end," he suggested, reaching for the book. "Maybe old Weird Willie fell smack in the middle of the mother lode and hid his fortune here in the house."

"That wasn't his name," she said with a quick laugh, holding the journal away from him. "And I've seen you with these old books. Once you open them, you don't get anything else done. You'll start reading and want to take it home with you."

Her laugh turned to a breathless protest as he leaned across her, gently pinning her to the back of the sofa and reaching for the book. "No, Brady," she said, striving for a firm tone. "Just because you want it, doesn't mean that you can have it."

His gaze veered from the book to her face. "Is that right?" he asked softly, his breath warm on her lips.

Sara's eyes widened nervously. "That's right," she whispered.

He bent his head forward, brushing the tip of his tongue against her full, lower lip. When both his lips covered hers, it wasn't in the hard, demanding kiss that Sara expected. Instead, they moved softly, persuasively over hers. That was even more dangerous, she thought vaguely, stiffening in protest. A woman just couldn't defend herself against something that . . . insidious.

Brady lifted his head a fraction of an inch and smiled down at her. "You can relax, honey. I told you once, I don't grab."

Taking advantage of that one small respite, Sara worked her hands up between them. They were both too preoccupied to notice Zak shamble over to an instrument behind them and flip a lever.

A barrage of thundering, dissonant sounds almost shattered their eardrums. It also brought Sara's faltering words to a standstill. Since she had no idea what she planned to say next, she thought it was nothing less than an answer to her prayers.

As Brady turned away to face the cacophony, it segued into something reminiscent of an 1880s barroom. "What in holy hell is that racket?"

He broke off as he faced Zak. Complete with derby and white cuffs, the ape was sitting on a low stool before a player piano. Pumping pedals for all he was worth, he slid the derby to the back of his head and grinned at Brady. Reaching out one long arm to a nearby table, Zak grabbed an apple and popped it into his mouth. After a minimum of chewing and one swallow, he extended his mobile lower lip and looked down with cross-eyed concentration to examine the remains. Apparently satisfied that he hadn't missed anything, he hastily swallowed what was left.

Brady's muffled oath was lost somewhere between the swell of music and Sara's giggle. A reluctant, one-sided curve of his lips twitched his mustache. With an audible groan of resignation, he said, "I don't remember that particular scene in any of his films."

"It's for the one coming up," Sara said with obvious amusement. "As far as I can tell, it's about a traveling circus in the old West."

Zak continued playing with all the zest and panache of a seasoned performer.

"Is it ever going to end?" Brady asked politely after a few minutes.

"Eventually. Those rolls seem to go on forever."

Watching as Zak ran a long finger down the keys in a silent trill that was a few seconds late—at least it was if he was trying to synchronize it with the music—Brady thought of Tabitha. He was going to have to talk with her. Again. The first time, it had been about Zak's animosity. She had the answer, she'd assured him. Propinquity. It worked every time. Zak was a lovable lad and the more time he spent with a person the fonder he became of him. So he had spent every spare moment at Sara's house with Tabitha running interference between him and a sulky Zak. Eventually the ape had quit spearing tree trunks at him and trying to forcibly eject him every time he ventured too near to Sara. In fact, after a week or so Zak apparently decided Brady meant Sara no harm and became quite devoted to him.

That had been the object of the second talk—Zak's overenthusiastic demonstrations of affection. He didn't like being kissed by a monkey, he'd informed Tabitha. Or an ape. Tabitha promised she would try. But it was harder to turn Zak off than it was to turn him on. However, whatever she'd done had worked fairly well. Now Zak merely subjected him to affectionate glances and an occasional hug.

Brady could visualize Tabitha's exasperation if he requested that she confine her charge to quarters occasionally. And he could understand her concern. Zak was like an overgrown child who had always had the run of the house. Probably, he decided, glancing down to enjoy Sara's smile, the best approach would be to appeal to Tabitha's matchmaking efforts. It would be hard on Zak, he acknowledged, but in a desperate situation such as this, it was every man for himself.

Sara pointed to the bulky manila envelope he had placed on the table. "What do you have in there?"

Brady reached over and silently unwound the slender cord at the back. Tilting the package, he withdrew a sheaf of photographs. Sara leaned forward and studied them, a thoughtful frown furrowing two vertical lines between her russet brows.

Brady didn't move, his eyes intent on her expressive face. At that moment, he realized, he yearned for his camera almost as much as he wanted Sara. It was a feeling that he should be accustomed to, he thought wryly. At their first meeting, even as he tackled her to the ground and covered her body with his, he had unconsciously and automatically blocked out shots, catching the glory of her hair against the lush green lawn. As far as that went, he decided, there wasn't a person, or animal, in the house who wasn't camera-worthy. What he needed was at least a month and about a thousand rolls of film.

There was a definite possibility, however, that the others would be shortchanged. It would take more than a month, probably forever, to record all the facets of this woman. He wanted Sara in the morning, drowsy and well loved. Sara entertained, fascinated, puzzled, amused and annoyed. Definitely annoyed, he decided, remembering the blast of energy emanating from her when she was ticked off. He wanted Sara in jeans, in that subtle-but-sexy black jumpsuit, and he wanted her with absolutely nothing on at all.

Sara looked up from her study of the pictures. "When did you take these?" She broke off with a curious glance. His eyes were on her in a rather abstracted manner, his mind obviously far away. With a feeling that she was interrupting some very pleasant mental digressions, she tapped his knee with a photo. "Anyone home?" she inquired.

Brady blinked. Sara was watching him, waiting patiently for an answer.

Sighing, she repeated, "When did you take these?"

"Before you moved in."

"It seems that you and Nicholas have something in common."

"Not at all. It was perfectly legal."

"How do you figure that? All the owners were several hundred miles away, and none of them gave you permission to take pictures."

"Do you mind?" he inquired.

"Not really. Not now. I'd just like to know how and why you did it."

Brady shuffled through the pictures, selected a few and spread them face up on the table. "After you bought the house, my aunt told me about the changes and renovations you planned. She said you had a genuine interest in old homes. She also grudgingly admitted that the changes weren't going to be too bad."

"Big of her," Sara said dryly.

"That's Aunt Helene. All heart."

"The pictures," Sara prompted.

"Right. Originally, I was interested because our houses are the same. My ancestors had done a fair job of keeping journals; I thought I could add a pictorial chapter. So I went through the house and shot everything the way it was before the workers started hacking away."

Holding up a hand, Sara said, "Craftsmen. And they didn't hack. How did you get in?"

"I went to school with Al, the contractor. When I told him what I wanted to do, he came out and let me in."

Sara stared at him in disbelief. "How accommodating. How did he know I wouldn't mind?"

Not about to tell her that Al would have cooperated with him even if she had, Brady said soothingly, "This isn't Los Angeles, Sara. My uncle lived here. I spent most of my summer vacations with him. They knew I could be trusted. Besides," he pointed out reasonably, "you were the outsider. Everyone knows this place belonged to my family. Now, do you want to hear the rest of this or not?"

After raising her eyes to the ceiling for a brief but heartfelt moment, she sighed. "Go on."

"The more I shot, the more I thought of the new owner," he laced his fingers through hers, lifted her hand and dropped a swift kiss on the tip of her index finger, "and the more I decided the photographs would make a nice house gift."

"Really?" she asked, quick pleasure lighting her eyes.

"Yep. Sort of a welcome-to-the-neighborhood present. So here it is, a step-by-step coverage of all the work. Ready to pass on to the next interested person with all the written material."

She squeezed his hand. "This is wonderful. Thank you. I want to see them all. Which ones did you take first? Did the workmen think you were crazy?"

Answering the last question first, he shook his head. "No. They're all artists in their own way and love these old places. In fact, they'd call me if they were ready to start something and thought I should be here." He rejected the coffee table as a work site. "We should spread these out so there's some measure of continuity."

Sara stood up. "Why don't we use the dining-room table?"

"Good." He looked around at Zak, who was still pedaling and creating a cheerful din. He was also peeling a banana. "Maybe we can get away from the maestro here."

"For a while. As soon as he's done, he'll come looking for us," she predicted, leading the way to the other room.

"Brady, these are really wonderful," Sara said slowly, looking down at the photos covering the tabletop. "You must have spent hours taking them."

Nodding matter-of-factly, he said, "I did."

"I don't know how to thank you."

Looking down at her absorbed expression, he said quietly, "Your pleasure is enough."

Sara glanced up, smiling tentatively. She realized belatedly that she had given him a perfect opening for some machismo response. But she shouldn't be surprised that he had bypassed the obvious, she reminded herself. Although Brady bristled with masculinity, or perhaps because of it, Sara pondered, he never came across as a chest-thumping male. As he had informed her, he didn't grab. But he issued sensual invitations that were almost impossible to decline. And he was subtle. All in all, a most dangerous man, she decided.

In irritation she wondered why they couldn't just remain friends, companions. Why did things have to reach the point where intimacy and commitment were next in the natural progression of events?

Probably because those two words, *friends* and *companions*, were anemic, bloodless expressions compared to the relationship Brady was after. He had told her what he wanted. Lord, he had almost shouted it from the tops of the surrounding mountains. He'd even given her a *deadline*, for heaven's sake!

And because Brady wasn't a eunuch, she told herself. He was a vital man, too attractive for his own good—and hers. Not a handsome or gorgeous man. Just . . . attractive.

Unfortunately, he was dealing with a woman who had a memory like an elephant's. She knew what it felt like to have her fingers—and her heart—burned. Once, in the midst of her pain, she had declared

SILHOUETTE GIVES YOU SIX REASONS TO CELEBRATE!

INCLUDING:

1.
4 FREE BOOKS

2.
AN ELEGANT MANICURE SET

3.
A SURPRISE BONUS

AND MORE!

TAKE A LOOK . . .

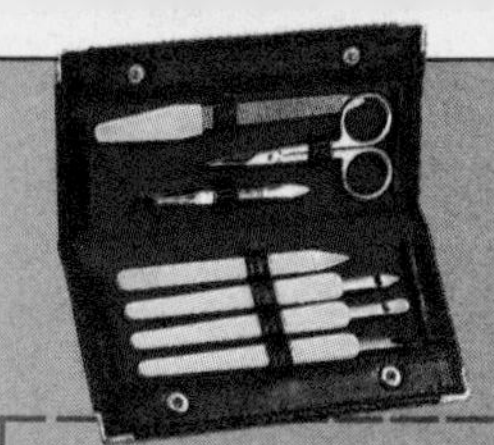

This beautiful manicure set will be a useful and elegant item to carry in your handbag. Its rich burgundy case is a perfect expression of your style and good taste. And it's yours free in this amazing Silhouette celebration!

SILHOUETTE ROMANCE®

FREE OFFER CARD

4 FREE BOOKS

ELEGANT MANICURE SET —FREE

FREE MYSTERY BONUS

PLACE YOUR BALLOON STICKER HERE!

FREE HOME DELIVERY

FREE FACT-FILLED NEWSLETTER

MORE SURPRISE GIFTS THROUGHOUT THE YEAR—FREE

Yes! Please send me my four Silhouette Romance novels **FREE,** along with my manicure set and my **free mystery gift.** Then send me six new Silhouette Romance novels every month and bill me just $1.95 per book, with no extra charges for shipping and handling. If I am not completely satisfied, I may return a shipment and cancel at any time. **The free books, manicure set and mystery gift remain mine to keep.**

CBR017

NAME ____________________

(PLEASE PRINT)

ADDRESS ____________________ APT. ________

CITY ____________________ STATE ________

ZIP ____________________

Terms and prices subject to change.
Your enrollment is subject to acceptance by Silhouette Books.

SILHOUETTE "NO RISK GUARANTEE"

- There is no obligation to buy—the free books and gifts remain yours to keep.
- You receive books before they're available in stores.
- You may end your subscription anytime—just let us know.

PRINTED IN U.S.A.

Remember! To receive your four free books, manicure set and surprise mystery bonus, return the postpaid card below. But don't delay!

DETACH AND MAIL CARD TODAY

If card has been removed, write to: Silhouette Books
120 Brighton Road, P.O. Box 5084, Clifton, NJ 07015-9956

NO POSTAGE
NECESSARY
IF MAILED
IN THE
UNITED STATES

BUSINESS REPLY MAIL
FIRST CLASS PERMIT NO. 194 CLIFTON, N.J.

Postage will be paid by addressee

SILHOUETTE BOOKS
120 Brighton Road
P.O. Box 5084
Clifton, NJ 07015-9956

sweepingly that all men were bastards and not to be trusted. Later, she'd known she was wrong, had even admitted it. But that didn't alter the fact that she was understandably leery about placing her hand over a flame.

Looking back down at the photos, she prodded one of the kitchen cupboard. Where was all this going, she wondered in agitation, a frown drawing her brows together. How could a woman who wanted no part of commitments cope with a man who seemed to handle them so easily? How could a woman with a damaged trusting mechanism deal with a man who demanded trust? And, more to the point, how could a woman—how could *she*—turn away from such a man when her very blood and bones called out to him?

"These will be perfect for the section on restoration," she murmured, hardly knowing what she was saying. "Has your aunt seen them?"

He shook his head. "No. She knew I had taken them, though."

"You do have your uses, don't you?" she asked, striving for a light tone.

"I try. Sara?"

Startled by the seriousness of his tone, she glanced up. Brady reached out and drew her to him. His hands curved around her neck beneath the softly scented fall of her dark red hair. His thumbs gently pressed upward on her chin. Agitation leaped from her eyes.

"Brady, I don't think—"

The warm touch of his lips swallowed the rest of her words. When he raised his head, she tried again.

"Brady, I—"

This time his thumb softly stroked her lips. "Honey," he said, his voice little more than a murmur, "I can think of many words that describe you but *coward* isn't one of them."

Her eyes widened in surprise, then closed as he bent his head and once again covered her mouth with his.

Over the roar of her blood, Sara almost missed his whisper.

"Trust me, Sara."

Later, long after he had gone, she still heard his softly spoken words.

Chapter Six

Hi, Emily, have you seen Zak?'' Sara poked her head in the doorway of the small sun room where Emily was lingering over her morning cup of coffee, reading the newspaper. Pale sunlight filtered through the lace curtains of the bay window.

Emily looked around. ''No. Maybe he's with Tabitha. She mentioned she wanted to work with him this morning.''

''I know. That's why I'm looking for him.''

Emily's eyes drifted back to the paper spread before her. ''Have you checked Billy's room? He bought a new hat yesterday.''

''Oh, God. Thanks. See you later.''

Emily nodded, already engrossed in the printed deluge of murders, swindles and spies.

''I found him,'' Sara announced in a few minutes. ''Trying to open Billy's door. Is there any good news?" she asked, sitting down across the table from Emily. She moved a section of the paper aside and replaced it with her mug of steaming coffee.

"The condors in California are doing better."

"That's nice." Sara's heart really wasn't with almost-extinct birds this morning.

"But they're all in zoos."

"That's awful! Anything else?"

"That spy was convicted."

"Good."

"A woman won a million dollars at a dollar slot machine in Reno."

Sara watched Emily's lips moving, but what she heard was a man's husky whisper saying, "Trust me." "It isn't easy to do," Sara said with feeling, adding cream to her coffee.

"Sheer luck, of course," Emily said, puzzled. Narrowing her eyes, she added, "I thought you gave up sugar in your coffee."

"I did," Sara said, absently dropping in her third spoonful.

"Just wondered," Emily said, giving her paper a shake and using it as a shield. "There's a big write-up about women being exploited."

Sara nodded. "Probably trusted the wrong person. I mean people," she added quickly, lifting the mug to her mouth and swallowing. Staring in affront at the syrupy mess, she asked, "Is your coffee all right?"

"Just fine," Emily replied serenely, reading the rest of the article. "It talks about the marketplace and the disproportionate number of men to women in executive positions. And how the skills of some women in subordinate positions are being used by others, of both sexes, who are on their way up the corporate ladder. That's where the exploitation comes in."

"Hah! You see? Just what I said," Sara declared. "Those women, the exploited ones, trusted the wrong people. They haven't learned how to take care of themselves yet."

Both women fell silent—Sara to follow her own particularly gloomy train of thought and Emily to turn the pages as she pursued the rest of the article. Sara finished her coffee in grumpy silence. On her way to the door she said, "By the way, Emily, Brady mentioned he's working on a big spread for one of the magazines. There's going to be a regular parade going out to his place. So if any of the beautiful people knock on the door, you know where to send them."

"Uh-hmm." The older woman lifted her head, an arrested look on her round face. "Talk about exploited women. Those girls are—"

"Doing exactly what they want to be doing," Sara interrupted. "It's the last word I'd apply to them. Their beauty is a commodity and they're being well paid for it, so don't waste your sympathy on them."

"Uh-hmm."

Sara left, momentarily distracted by Emily's noncommittal response. But before she had taken three steps, her mind had shifted to the enormous commission before her. She had known all along that some day the pleasant task of research would have to give way to the actual process of writing. Research was by no means over; she still had most of the collection at Brady's to sift through, but today was D day. She had declared the day be set aside for writing. And just to reinforce her decision, she told everyone who had even the slightest interest in the project. Smiling faintly, she envisioned words forming well-constructed sentences and paragraphs, flowing onto one page after another.

After an hour in the makeshift office, her smile had faded. A small storage room had been cleared out for her use, and a large desk and two-drawer standing file had been moved in. Filling up the other corners were boxes of books and photos from the attic. And, sitting smack in the middle of the desk, was the new typewriter. Sara glanced down at it in disgust. So far, it hadn't typed one solitary word by itself. And she had arrived at the disheartening conclusion that it wasn't going to.

A book, she discovered, was not easy to write. This hadn't surprised her; she'd always had a sneaking suspicion that it might not be as simple as it looked. Her years of laboring over monthly newsletters had left her with few literary illusions—or aspirations. Mumbling beneath her breath at Helene Felton's steamrolling tactics and her own inability to cope with them, Sara leaned back and glared at the typewriter. "First paragraph," she muttered. "At least get the first paragraph."

Three hours later, leaning forward with her elbows propped on the typewriter, Sara scowled down at the paper. There, facing her, was the most god-awful, double-spaced mess of words she had ever seen. How many times, she wondered, can you describe a house as stately and gracious and get away with it? Not as many as she had, she decided gloomily. Obviously she had to make some minor revisions, change a few words here and there, or take them out completely. But if she eliminated those words, the sentences didn't make any sense. And if she eliminated the senseless sentences, there went the whole paragraph.

Before she could follow her impulse to rip the paper from the machine and toss it into the wastebasket, Sara was distracted by a quiet knock at the open door. She looked up and stared in surprise. Brady stood in the doorway.

"Hi," she said a little uncertainly. The last words he had said to her had been "Trust me." That had been several evenings ago. He'd been in Reno since then. So close and yet so very far away.

Brady leaned casually against the door frame, one ankle crossed over the other. He held a large, fussily wrapped box in his hand. "Brought you something," he said, grinning at her sudden look of wide-eyed expectation. It wasn't the look he was hoping to see, but it was far better than the wary expression that had crossed her face when she first glanced up.

He came in and perched on the corner of the desk, holding out the box.

Sara took it, weighing it in her hands. With a sudden smile that intensified the gold flecks in her eyes, she said, "If it's chocolates, I'm in trouble. It weighs a ton."

Brady watched as she tried to ease the ribbon over one of the corners. Almost four days, he thought hungrily, resisting the urge to haul her into his arms. Four days without seeing her smile or walk across a room. Four days of wondering if he'd been too optimistic with his Christmas deadline.

"A thesaurus! Brady, you darling! How did you know I'd come down with a terminal case of the blanks?" Sara's arm slipped around his neck in a quick hug. He draped his arm loosely around her waist, fighting the impulse to pull her against his aching body. But it was the first spontaneous gesture of affection—however platonic—she had made in his direction, and he wasn't about to blow it now.

"You have no idea how hard this whole thing is," she complained, greedily flipping the pages of the book. "Aha! Look at this," she commanded, reading aloud. "'Grand, dignified, proud, magnificent, palatial, splendid, resplendent, marvelous, regal, superb.' Isn't that wonderful? Now, maybe I can save my one and only paragraph," she said, glancing up with a laugh.

Brady looked down, grinning at her expression of smug satisfaction. He was not a prudent man. He'd made that discovery years before. But neither was he a fool. He wasn't about to admit that the book had been meant as a joke. He'd been determined to return with something for her, a nonverbal reminder that he had thought about her while he was gone. It hadn't been easy; he'd deliberately avoided personal items. He knew instinctively that anything along that line would bring back that guarded look to her lovely eyes. So he'd ended up in a bookstore, buying the most conservative thing in sight, something even his ancestors would have deemed an appropriate gift. And here she was, gloating over it as if it were a bagful of diamonds.

"How's it going?" he asked. "Have you decided to give Michener a run for his money?"

"Very funny," she said dryly. "Do you have any idea how many words it takes to fill up a page?"

"A lot?" he ventured.

"More than that. And you just can't use the same ones over and over, you have to keep dredging up new ones. And something else just occurred to me. I have a nasty feeling that Helene is going to suggest using a small print size, and that will mean even *more* words."

"Sounds like a losing proposition," he sympathized, humor lurking in his gray eyes. Before she could react to it, he asked, "How about using a lot of pictures? Between us, we've got enough for a ten-volume set."

"I'm counting on that," she assured him grimly. "And speaking of pictures, what are you doing here? I thought you were going to be up to your eyeballs in beautiful women today."

Brady glanced at his watch and said, "I will be in a couple of hours. The legs come first."

Sara thought about that for a moment. "Are they sending them out in sections now?"

His hand brushed her back and neck before it stopped in her thick hair. Tightening his fingers, he tugged lightly, raising her face to his. Dropping a quick kiss on the tip of her nose, he said, "No. Progress hasn't taken us to that point yet. They still come in one piece. I just take the parts I need. Stockings are first; therefore, legs."

With a reluctant sigh, he loosened his hold, fingering the last strand of hair as it slid from his hand. "See you tonight?" he inquired.

"How many more boxes do we still have to go through?"

"Four or five."

Sara sighed. "Tonight. What time will the last of the legs be gone?"

"Come about seven," Brady said before he turned his back to the typewriter and went out the door.

The rest of the afternoon passed quickly. In between bouts of sporadic typing, Sara wandered around the house muttering aloud and searching for inspiration. No one in the house came near her; Tabitha even kept Zak away. The only distractions were distant ones. Occasionally the doorbell rang. Once, in response to the sound, she walked to the door only to find Emily in the driveway, talking emphatically and pointing, apparently giving a lost model directions to Brady's house.

Sara loaded Zak in Tabitha's truck again that evening. Tabitha had been oddly reluctant to let Zak accompany her, but Sara had insisted. No, it wasn't odd at all, she decided, after giving it some thought. Tabitha was doing her matchmaking number again, and wanted to deprive her of a chaperon. Not that Zak was doing such a hot job in that direction. Each time he went to Brady's, he patted the man affectionately on the shoulder, tried to sneak a kiss, and disappeared. But he was better than nothing. If things reached an awkward stage, she could always wonder aloud where he was and instigate a search.

"Things aren't getting any easier," she told Zak. He looked up alertly and reached out to touch her hand. Brady was a bit like an avalanche, she thought. It didn't matter what obstacles were in his way, he just battered them down and kept on coming. She had tried cool disinterest, a display of temper, and calm explanations, but nothing worked. He was neither discouraged nor ready to abandon his efforts. Every time he was with her, he tacitly reaffirmed his position. He wanted her and intended to have her.

"Why can't I be like other women?" she asked Zak plaintively. Why couldn't she just go to bed with the man? Other single women managed it without damaging their psyches. Why on earth couldn't she? Because, she reminded herself, after a couple of awkward experiences following her divorce, she'd learned she was constitutionally unsuited for affairs.

Sara frowned into the lights of an oncoming car and lowered the high beams. Of course, that had all been a long time ago. Maybe she could handle it now. Her inept attempts to prove that she was still an attractive woman had taken place during that first traumatized year of finding herself single again. A lot of things had changed since then. *She* had changed. She no longer had to prove herself. She knew exactly who and what she was. Unfortunately, what she was, was a woman lusting after a man who scared her silly.

Slumping back in the seat, Sara absentmindedly flipped the high beams back on. All right, she had admitted it. She had never known a man who made her feel so much a woman. She wanted his arms around her, she wanted his lips and body on hers, and she wanted everything that would normally follow. She wanted him in bed, in front of the fireplace or in the middle of his hot tub. So, what now? she asked herself. What was she going to do about it? What did she do with the woman living inside her body who wanted Brady Cameron? Did she satisfy her, or did she dunk her in a tub of cold water?

Putting aside the thought of cold water for the moment, Sara considered the other available options. He was certainly open with her. Why couldn't she be the same? She could spend the night with Brady and hope that one night would rid her of the obsession—assuming of course that she didn't turn craven at the last moment. And if one night didn't do it? Or two, even three? Was forty-four too old for a full-fledged affair? Sara sighed, thinking of her five elderly friends who took such an active interest in her life. A discreet affair? There was no such animal. At least, not around here. They'd know the minute they saw her face.

So much for options, she thought grouchily. Cold water, a one-night stand or an affair. At least Brady wasn't fool enough to ask for commitments. He read her well enough to know that she wanted no part of lifetime promises. She might be a bit shaky about handling a one-night fling, but she was absolutely certain that she wanted no part of the trust and involvement of marriage. Then, having settled nothing except her stand on permanent commitments, she pulled up into Brady's driveway and doused the lights.

The door opened before she even touched the bell. Brady dropped an arm around her shoulder and urged her inside.

"Are the legs gone?" she asked.

"Every last one of them," he said with satisfaction. Holding up a key ring packed with keys, he dangled it in front of Zak. "Here's a present," he told the ape, dropping the keys into his extended hand.

"What's that for?" Sara asked, watching as Zak closed his hand around the keys and waddled off.

"Billy told me how Zak's always trying to break into his room, so I thought I'd see how good he is at it. My ancestors apparently believed that every door should have a lock. The keys were kept in a drawer in that hall stand, so I pulled them out and locked all the doors. That should keep him entertained."

And busy, she added silently, scrutinizing his bland expression. Walking ahead of him, she stopped in the middle of the living room, drawn by its warmth and welcome. Each time she entered this room it was the same. The glow from the fire burning in the stone hearth, the soft lighting from the lamps and Brady's presence all delivered the same message: she was home; this was where she belonged. Shrugging uncomfortably, she reminded herself once again that this room was a duplicate of her own. It wasn't surprising that she should feel so contented here.

In an attempt to break the spell being woven around her, Sara knelt by one of the boxes and reached inside for a book. She knew the exact moment that Brady sat on the floor beside her, but she kept her eyes on the page before her.

Brady broke the extended silence with a sudden exclamation. "You've got to read this!" he told her, holding up a tattered journal. "Come here." Drawn by his excitement, she moved beside him. "Not there," he objected. "The light's not good enough." Patting the floor in front of him, he said, "Here."

Sara moved hesitantly, watching dubiously as he shifted his legs, leaning back against the sofa. She was drawn into the cradle between his thighs, her back against his chest, and after a long moment her head settled on his shoulder. Brady's arms wrapped around her and he unceremoniously deposited the open book in her lap. "Look at this," he commanded.

Easy for him to say, she thought indignantly. Surrounded by him, caught in the gentle trap of his warmth and scent, she couldn't make out a word written on the page. Taking a deep breath didn't help at all; it only made her more aware of the taut muscles of his legs and chest and the fact that he had recently showered. The very air around her was a heady combination of spicy after-shave and clean male.

Sara blinked and tried to focus on the writing. Instead, her eyes settled on the backs of his hands—tanned, strong, with a sprinkling of dark hair.

"Do you see it?"

His impatient query startled her, drawing her eyes hurriedly back to the book. "Just a minute."

Sara read quickly, at one point brushing his fingers aside to bring the book closer. Concentrating on the material before her, she relaxed, shifting comfortably against him. With her knees bent inside the framework of his, she fit against the contour of his body like a spoon.

Glancing up, she met his expectant gaze. Her own was replete with satisfaction. "This is perfect! What a story it makes."

Brady kept his response casual, with difficulty. He was far more aware of Sara's body than her conversation. "We aim to please," he managed tautly, grabbing a couple of pillows as the couch slid away behind him on the polished floor.

"Let me get this straight," she said, turning fractionally to face him, following him down as he sank back on the pillows. She propped her bent elbow on his chest and rested her cheek on her hand. "Your ancestor, great-great-great whatever he was, had twin sons. They got married at the same time and, for a wedding present, he built them each a house." She tapped his shoulder with a tapered finger. "Yours and mine."

Brady nodded. Closing his eyes briefly, he wondered if she knew what she was doing to him. She didn't, he decided, glancing up at her intrigued expression. Yet. She was too wrapped up in the past to be concerned about the present. But it wouldn't be long before she was jolted into awareness, he thought wryly. In fact, he gave her ten seconds at the outside.

"This is fantastic," she enthused. "Just the sort of thing I've been looking for. It gives a touch of romance and personality to the story—much more interesting than plain facts. What we've got to do, though," she told him briskly, "is get the rest of the stuff in chronological order. We've got to find out what happened to those two."

The book slid off Brady's chest to the floor. Sara leaned forward, across him, to pick it up. Her hand brushed from his hip to thigh then back again before she said, "There! I've got it. Now, all we need is—"

Brady stirred, his body twitching in an uncontrolled, reflexive movement. The involuntary movement of his body against the curve of her waist made a resounding statement of masculinity. Startled, Sara froze. Her voice broke off and she stared at the book, refusing to meet his eyes. After a heartbeat of silence, she burst into nervous chatter. "Oh, God, Brady, I'm sorry. I didn't mean to... We're not kids, we know better...I'll get up—"

"Sara," he said, his arms settling around her, holding her firmly to him, "if you value my sanity, you won't budge—not an inch." His lips were tilted in a rueful, one-sided smile. "And you're right, we're not kids. So just stay where you are."

It was one thing, Sara thought vaguely, to contemplate jumping into bed with him. It was another thing entirely to be confronted with reality, the masculine equivalent of an open invitation. Besides, when she had considered it, she had visualized how she would handle herself with poise and aplomb. She definitely wouldn't panic, stammer or try to run.

"Ah, Brady..."

"Honey, just let me hold you for a minute before you start arguing."

Sara heard the smile in his voice and was disarmed. The situation couldn't be too far out of hand if he could laugh about it, she reasoned. A moment later, she knew just how wrong she could be. Not quite certain how it happened, Sara found herself looking up at Brady as his head bent and his mouth settled on hers.

I'll straighten this out in a minute, she promised herself, wrapping her arms around his neck. Just another minute. His arms tightened, holding her closer and Sara shifted until her curves fit more comfortably against the hard planes of his body. Her sigh was a soft sound in her throat as his hand slipped down and cupped her softly rounded bottom.

Later, when Brady lifted his head, dazed hazel eyes searched determined gray ones.

In a husky whisper, Sara said, "Brady, don't play with me. I forgot the rules to this game a long time ago."

"Good, because I stopped playing a long time ago."

"When?"

"The first day I saw you."

"Well, it has been a lot longer than that for me. I'm not very good at this kind of stuff."

"Sara, darlin'," he drawled, a slow, utterly fascinating smile curving his lips, "if you were any better—"

"I mean I don't handle casual . . . encounters very well," she interrupted desperately, turning her face to avoid the touch of his lips.

"Good," he stated evenly, deliberately misunderstanding, "because there's nothing casual about this encounter at all."

"All I'm trying to say is—"

"That you're getting scared." His thumb pressed gently against her chin until she faced him again, her eyes meeting his. "You've removed yourself from the real world—"

"I have not!"

"—because someone hurt you. I'm making you feel like a woman again, and you don't like it."

Sara made a rude noise.

Brady's gaze held hers as he shifted, easing his weight off her even as his arms kept her captive. "I've seen it in your eyes, Sara. You can't hide it any more than I can. I'm in your blood exactly the way you're in mine. Every day it gets harder not to touch, to taste, to feel, doesn't it?"

Sara shook her head in denial, closing her eyes so they wouldn't betray her.

Brady went on, his voice relentless. "I know exactly how it is, because I want you so badly I ache. I want to feel your sweet, naked body against mine. I want to hold you so close that I can't tell where your body ends and mine begins. I want everything you have to give."

Clearing her dry throat, Sara said, "I have nothing to give."

"Only the world," he said, dropping a soft kiss on the wildly beating pulse in her throat. "But first, you have to take. If you're not afraid, honey, then reach out and take what you want."

The challenge was loud and clear, and for once his words weren't laced with humor. The expression on his face was one of sheer determination. What he was asking wasn't easy, he silently acknowledged, but with every muscle in his body, he urged her on.

Sara moved her head restlessly. "Brady," she began.

"Reach out, honey, that's all you have to do."

His whisper broke through ten years of restraint, ten years of hurting, healing, and waiting for life to resume. Her hands reached up and slowly laced through his dark hair. Tugging, she brought his head down and lifted her face to brush his lips with hers. His groan was all the encouragement she needed. Sliding her arms around his neck, she shifted until she lay alongside his body, melding soft curves to taut muscles. When a long tremor shuddered through her body, she collapsed bonelessly against him. Her slow, deeply feminine smile was one of satisfaction and contentment.

Sighing, she rested her head on his shoulder, tracing the contours of his face with her finger. "You were right," she admitted lazily, "I need you. I don't sleep at night because I miss you. And my days aren't any better."

His eyes never left hers. Was she really ready to make the commitment he needed?

Twining several strands of his hair around her finger, she said with a soft laugh, "Once, when you were in a rather imperious mood, you issued a deadline. You said I'd be in your bed by Christmas." Slanting a teasing look up at him, she said, "I don't think I can wait that long. I want you, Brady. Now."

The wary expression in his gray eyes and the sudden, coiling tension in his body almost prepared her for his chilling words. Almost.

"For how long?"

Sara blinked in confusion. "What?"

"How long will you need me, Sara. One night? Two?" he demanded.

Her smile faded as she slowly sat up and moved away, cutting herself off from his warmth. "I don't understand."

"I want more than that, honey."

Sara closed her eyes against the pain, then stood and buttoned her shirt. She cursed her trembling fingers. "I just offered you everything I have," she said with quiet pride.

"No you didn't." He rose in one quick movement and towered over her. "You have a lifetime of nights, a world of love to give. I want it all, Sara: marriage, a home, everything. I won't settle for less."

She raised her chin in protest.

He cut her off before she even began. "Sara, I'd give everything I own to take you upstairs tonight, and you know it. But I'm not going to jeopardize the rest of our lives for one night."

Expressionlessly she said, "I think I'd better go."

Brady watched as she put on her light jacket and called Zak. He leaned against the front door, blocking her way. "The deadline still stands."

"Goodbye, Brady." Her voice was cool, final.

"By Christmas you'll be my wife."

Chapter Seven

Brady's oath was soft and succinct as he closed the door behind him. The past week had not been one he cared to repeat. His schedule had been shot to hell, Zak had visited twice—alone, leaving his kitchen looking like a cornfield in the Midwest after a horde of locusts had descended—and he hadn't seen Sara in six days. Now, if the light at the end of the hall meant what he thought it did, Nicholas had bypassed his alarm system again.

He walked toward the light wondering precisely when the chaos had begun. His hand moved up, in what had become an automatic gesture, to massage the tight muscles in his neck. Even though it seemed to stem from the night Sara had walked out, her straight back radiating hurt pride and obstinacy, it had to be more than that. Models who had been punctual and efficient were arriving late and complaining about the length of the sessions. These were the same women who had previously begged their agents for commissions with him. And his house, which had always had the effect of alleviating his trials, now deafened him with its silence.

Nicholas looked up from the crossword puzzle with an abstracted nod.

"Don't let me interrupt you," Brady said, his words lightly veiled with sarcasm.

Nicholas penciled in a word and placed the paper beside him with a satisfied smile. "You're late tonight."

"Let's see," Brady said, pouring a small amount of brandy for himself and refilling Nicholas's glass, "is this the fourth or fifth time you've helped yourself to my brandy?"

"Sixth. But you're getting off easy. Think how much it would cost if I charged you. I don't come cheap," he reminded Brady.

Brady sat down in a chair across from him, a smile glimmering in his eyes at the picture of relaxed arrogance the older man made. "My security people are beginning to make disapproving noises. They're convinced that I leave without turning the system on."

"They're just trying to save face," Nicholas assured him. "They make the changes, don't they?"

Brady nodded. Nicholas knew they had; he'd inspected the work after it was done.

Nicholas shrugged. The movement said, "What can I say?" as clearly as if he had spoken.

A comfortable silence fell between the two men. Neither of them felt obligated to break it with a flow of words. They stared at the fire, each occupied with his own thoughts.

"Sara doesn't look happy," Nicholas said finally.

"Neither do I."

"I noticed." He waited patiently.

"I asked her to marry me." Brady considered his statement for a moment. "Well, actually, I told her she was going to marry me."

"Our Sara doesn't respond very well to orders."

"I noticed." He watched as the gleam of amusement in the other man's eyes grew stronger. "Damn it, Nick, she's willing to throw away everything we have between us just to avoid the possibility of getting hurt." He stood up and walked over to the fire. "I won't let her do it."

Nicholas nodded in approval. "Good."

"Is that all you've got to say?"

Nicholas nodded.

"No advice to the lovelorn? No quick solution?"

"No."

"Any words of comfort?"

Nicholas grinned and shook his head. "You don't need them. In the short time we've been here, you'vc managed to crack Sara's protective shell. That's more than any other man has done."

"There's something else I'd like to put a dent in," he stated grimly, thinking of her obstinate resistance. Sweet and stubborn, that covered the ground pretty thoroughly, he decided. From the top of her gleaming red head to her narrow, high-arched feet, Sara was an intriguing and irresistible challenge, one he'd known from the beginning would be troublesome, but well worth the effort involved.

He stretched out his legs, leaned back in the chair with an exasperated sigh and took a long, slow swallow of his drink. The resolute expression on his face did not soften. Damn it! Dealing with a woman like Sara, he couldn't afford to be soft. Not if he wanted to have her in his life on a permanent basis. Besides, she wasn't a woman who could sleep with a man one night and blithely walk away in the morning. She should know that. And since he was the man in question, she wouldn't be allowed the option of walking. She would learn that in quick order if she ever made the same offer again. And God help her if she did, because he wouldn't have the strength to let her leave a second time.

"Will she talk to you?" Nicholas looked at him questioningly.

"I don't know, I haven't given her the chance." He might be putting their collective futures on the line, but he wasn't a fool. He wasn't going to present her with the opportunity to close the door in his face or puncture an eardrum by slamming the telephone down before he had had his say. Instead, he had bundled up the journals and left them on her porch before dawn the day after she'd walked out of his house.

He hadn't slept that night. Memories of her soft, responsive body had kept him pacing the floor. Her breathless cries and her eyes, cautious at first, then quickly giving way to astonished hunger, haunted him. No, he hadn't had much sleep, that night or any since.

"What are you going to do?" Nicholas looked intrigued.

"Give her some time."

"To cool off?"

"And to think. Right now, she's probably knee-deep in reference books and journals. By the time she gets to the section on this latest reconstruction work and needs my help, she might be ready to talk to me."

Nicholas wondered. Considering Sara's closed expression and the intensity with which she was tackling Helene Felton's brainstorm, it might be several weeks before she decided to come up for air. In the meantime, perhaps he could do something to distract Brady. It was only fair, he decided. He had been the one who found the house and brought the others to see it. If Brady's problems arose from the move, it was only fair that he, Nicholas, should attempt to rectify them.

He reflected on the younger man's reaction to his nocturnal visits. It was more than concern about his security system. Although he complained mildly about the sinking level in the decanter of expensive brandy after each of the illicit sorties, he reacted with a certain amount of intrigued amusement. Yes, Nicholas decided, Brady would definitely be interested in his latest enterprise.

"Did I tell you about the place my company has been working on?" he asked casually. "They're installing some of the latest equipment in it."

"Around here?" Brady inquired with lazy interest.

"Up by Lake Tahoe."

"If your firm is involved, it must be a pretty big place."

"A respectable size," Nicholas admitted fairly, "on a decent estate."

Brady thoughtfully regarded the older man. He was becoming accustomed to Nicholas's deprecating figures of speech. What they were discussing, he decided, was probably a walloping mansion on a hundred acres.

"You don't mean that fortress dug into the mountain north of Zephyr Cover, by any chance?"

"You've seen it?" Nicholas asked, mildly surprised.

Brady studied him with knit brows. Nicholas was playing this one just a bit too coolly, he decided. Everyone within several hundred miles had seen it; it was a monstrosity that looked like a cross between Alcatraz and some gothic horror. In blatant warning to potential burglars, its security measures had been the subject of several front-page articles in the local papers.

He nodded. "You can hardly miss it," he said dryly.

"True," Nicholas agreed.

Brady regarded the other man with narrowed eyes. Nicholas was up to something. He was altogether too bland. If he had learned anything in their brief encounters, however, it was that Nicholas could not be prodded. He did everything in his own time. But that game could be played by more than one, he thought, settling back in his chair and gazing at the fire.

After a protracted silence, Nicholas stated, "The company has put all their latest equipment into the place. It's supposed to be foolproof."

"Hmm," Brady responded, closing his eyes.

"They should be done in several weeks."

"Really?"

"They say they don't need me to do a final run-through."

"Oh?"

Nicholas nodded. "The computerized system covers all the angles, so they say."

"Hmm."

"It monitors a heat sensor around the fence and yard area, plus all the electronic gadgets in the house."

"Ah."

"It looks good on paper, I must admit."

"Good."

"But they forgot one thing."

Brady's spine stiffened and he opened one eye. He had a feeling that Nicholas was about to drop the other shoe. "What?" he asked cautiously.

"Nothing is foolproof," he said with a slow smile. "There's always a way to get in. It just has to be found."

"Oh, God," Brady groaned, watching the smile broaden on the other man's face. "I don't want to hear any more."

"Once they give it a final check, I'm going in." Nicholas spoke quietly but with absolute certainty.

"The hell you are!" Brady ran an agitated hand through his hair.

"And I'll get out without anyone being the wiser."

"Nicholas—"

"Don't worry," he soothed, "I won't disturb anyone."

"You mean the people are *living* there?"

Nicholas gave an absent nod. "They've been in residence for a couple of weeks."

"Listen, Nick—"

"With their guard-trained Dobermans."

"Oh, hell!" Brady swore in frustration. "You wouldn't even be going in under the auspices of your firm this time. Have you ever heard of something called 'breaking and entering'?"

Nicholas shook his head, frowning slightly. "You and Sara," he chided gently, "are certainly a pessimistic pair. She's asked me the same question on more than one occasion." Pulling a piece of paper out of his pocket, he said, "Before I forget, pass this on to Landis so they can plug up your latest hole."

Brady reached out and took the note. Landis and company already had an active dislike for these memos. Another one would make their day. He jammed it in his shirt pocket and scowled across the few feet separating the two chairs.

Nicholas lowered his lids to conceal the amusement lurking there. Brady was proving to be just as stubborn as Sara had been in the past, he thought, observing the man who was looking more obstructive with each passing moment. Yes, he had been right, he congratulated himself. He couldn't have found a better way to divert him.

"Don't think you're going to change the subject that easily," Brady warned.

Nicholas's smile was deliberately annoying. "Are you going to issue dire warnings?" he murmured imperturbably.

"You're damned right I am!" Brady leaned forward and glared. "Do you have any idea how big a hole a Doberman can make in you?"

"It's immaterial," Nicholas said with a flick of his hand. "They never get that close."

"Not yet. There's always a first time."

"I should have kept a scrapbook," Nicholas sighed. "Then perhaps you'd believe that I know what I'm doing."

"A book like that would be a problem in your field," Brady conceded politely, "considering that publicity usually means that an intruder has been apprehended. But that's beside the point. It doesn't really matter what I think."

Nicholas inclined his head, matching the other man's civility. "In this particular case it does."

Brady eyed him suspiciously. "Why?" he asked bluntly.

Nicholas allowed the corners of his mouth to tilt in a small smile. "Because I thought you might like to come along."

Brady closed his eyes, recalling his peaceful life just three short months before. There had been no animal trainer pursuing an ape through his house, no sawed-off cowboy dropping ropes over his shoulders, no stockbroker sneering at his portfolios, no grandmotherly type lecturing on the wicked ways of the modern world, and no aging cat-burglar extending invitations to traipse through heavily secured, occupied fortresses. Nor had there been Sara. But now there was. And although nothing had been said, he knew if he took Sara, the others came as a bonus. It was definitely a package deal.

He opened his eyes to find Nicholas regarding him with a quizzical look. His smile had broadened.

"Well?"

"Do I look crazy?" Brady asked.

Nicholas tilted his head and examined him with thoughtful eyes. "No," he finally said.

"Does that answer your question?" He waited while Nicholas eyed him from head to toe.

"You've kept in shape," he observed. "Ever do any mountain climbing?"

The question took Brady by surprise. "Some," he allowed cautiously. "Why?"

"Rappeling."

The succinct word seemed to be all the explanation Nicholas had to offer.

"Rappeling?" Brady repeated, with all the suspicion of a wolf sniffing a baited trap. "As in sliding down ropes?" His misgivings grew as the other man nodded affably. "Why?"

"We have to get in," Nicholas said reasonably.

"Why not by helicopter?" It was no more absurd than ropes and pitons.

Nicholas regarded him with an expression usually reserved for a teacher evaluating a dim-witted student. "Too noisy."

"A pack of snarling, slavering Dobermans isn't exactly quiet," Brady commented dryly. His brows peaked in sudden inquiry as he puzzled over the question of mountain climbing. "Let's get back to the business of rappeling," he suggested. "Were you serious?"

"Of course." Nicholas gazed at him with a benign expression. "I never joke about business."

Brady closed his eyes and sighed. "All right," he said abruptly. "Let's just assume that we're taking this whole thing seriously." He glared at Nicholas, who nodded. "We're going to rappel down to the house, right?"

"Right."

"What in the name of God are we rappeling *from*?"

"The overhang of the mountain ledge above the house."

The silence in the room was finally broken by Brady's abrupt words. "You're crazy, Nick. You are stark, raving certifiable. I don't know why someone hasn't wrapped one of Billy Bob's ropes around you and carted you off." At the sight of the older man's amused smile, his words grew even shorter. "How far above the house is this convenient overhanging mountain ledge?"

"Two hundred feet, give or take forty or fifty," Nicholas said promptly.

"I don't believe it. You want to dangle two hundred feet from a probably faulty ledge—"

"It's perfectly stable. I've been up there."

"—and slide down to the—"

"Roof of the fourth-floor tower."

"—where, if you miss the Dobermans, you'll probably fall into a moat teeming with alligators."

Nicholas shook his head, visibly entertained. "Where do you get these exaggerated ideas? You have no idea how tedious and uneventful most of these trips are."

"Why can't you start on the ground floor?" Brady asked reasonably.

"Dobermans, heat sensors, electric eyes," Nicholas said rapidly, ticking them off on his fingers. "Need any more?"

"But why a fourth-floor tower?"

"Because," Nicholas murmured with a quick grin of savage satisfaction, "the fools didn't wire it."

Brady blinked. "How do you know?"

"I've seen the plans. In fact, I have a copy of them in my room."

Feeling like a straight man in a bad comedy routine, Brady asked, "Why didn't they wire it?"

"Because they didn't believe that anyone could get to it."

"Sounds reasonable to me," Brady muttered. "How is it that you have the plans?"

A reminiscent smile played over the other man's mouth. "They were so proud of their computerized innovations, they pulled them out and showed them to me. When they told me flat out that the wiring was burglarproof, I made admiring noises. They actually gave me a copy so I could study them and understand how the computer was going to put an end to burglaries." He shook his head at their gullibility.

Brady stared at him in disbelief. "They actually just handed them over to you?"

"They probably felt sorry for the old man past his prime," Nicholas said calmly. "Decided to give me a toy to play with as a consolation prize."

The security people were obviously a pack of prize idiots, Brady decided as he examined the amused expression on Nicholas's face. Or Nicholas was as good an actor as he was a housebreaker. He probably was, he decided after another quick glance. His mustache tilted as he visualized a bent old man walking out the door with a roll of schematics under his arm.

"When did you start planning this, uh, heist?"

Nicholas winced. "Please," he murmured, obviously pained. "Infiltration. Or penetration. I never take anything. At least, not for the past few years—and damned dull it is, too. But, in answer to your question, I began that very day. It was shortly after we moved here. For about the past month I've just been waiting for them to finish the job."

"How do you know they haven't made some modifications since they handed you the plans?" Brady asked curiously.

"They have made a few. But I've kept in touch with them, so I know what they've done." His quick grin jolted Brady. "They still think the tower is invulnerable."

"A company man would let them know it isn't," Brady commented.

Nicholas nodded agreeably. "So he would. But I've always thought that they must live incredibly dull lives."

Much like prudent men, Brady reflected. He got up as if he had been stung and walked over to the fireplace, stunned by the thought. He was a law-abiding man, always had been and probably always would be. He had no desire to feel the hot breath of a Doberman on his neck or to be hauled away in handcuffs by the local police.

Glancing over his shoulder at Nicholas, he groaned beneath his breath. The aging delinquent's bright, alert gaze met his. Neither man blinked. Nicholas would proceed with his plans regardless of Brady's decision. Both men knew that. Nothing Brady could say at this point would change his mind.

Shrugging, Brady returned to his chair. He sat down and stretched out his legs. Nicholas remained motionless, watching as the younger man frowned in thought.

He had some time in which to appeal to Nicholas's common sense, Brady told himself. He might just swing it. He probably wouldn't, he admitted realistically, but he had to try. And the only way he could do it would be to keep the door open. If he refused point-blank to join Nicholas, that would be that. Nick would leave and never mention the subject again. If, on the other hand, he expressed a certain amount of interest, the door would remain open for discussion.

And some fast talking was definitely in order. Sara's attachment to Nicholas was obvious. If anything happened to him and Sara found out that he had known of the older man's plans... He stopped, deciding that he didn't even want to examine that possibility.

"When did you say you were going?" he asked, striving for a casual tone.

Nicholas brightened. "In about three weeks."

"I still think it's a lunatic idea."

Nicholas checked the knifelike crease in his pants and crossed one knee over the other. He leaned back and waited. Patience was, after all, a characteristic necessary to his trade.

Heaving a sharp sigh, Brady said, "I'm not saying I'll do it, but I have to admit I'm damned curious about how *you're* going to swing the whole thing. Will you tell me?"

"I'll do better than that," Nicholas assured him with a satisfied smile. "I'll bring the plans over tomorrow night." He rose to his feet and, silently as a shadow, left the room.

* * *

Sara nodded in satisfaction as she read the last paragraph. Yes, that was it, exactly the tone she had striven for. Then, with a start she looked up from the humming typewriter and stared at the ringing telephone. Her heart did a quick flip. It might be Brady, her traitorous mind signaled hopefully. Saying he was sorry, of course, it hastily amended. It had been a week since she had ordered her wobbly legs to carry her out of his house. A week since he had told her flat out that what she offered wasn't enough; he wanted more. The blasted man *always* wanted more. First it was "You're going to be in my arms, my home and my bed—before Christmas." Now it was marriage—also before Christmas.

She glared as the telephone pealed again. She picked up the receiver and was almost relieved to hear Helene Felton's brisk voice.

"How are you doing on the book?"

Typical of the woman, she thought. No "Hello," no "How are you?" no "Do you need any help?" Sara looked upward, clearly begging for patience.

"You'll be relieved to know that I've just finished the historical part," she said—by staying up most of the night reading and working from dawn until after dark every day for a solid week, she added silently. Assuming correctly that the older woman wouldn't care about such insignificant details, she continued, speaking quickly before she could be interrupted. "Are you sure you want the section about the remodeling and restoration work we did when we bought the house? It seems to me that people would be more interested in the original building than recent modifications." And she wouldn't have to collaborate with Brady.

Helene didn't even allow her a moment of hope. "Sara! What *can* you be thinking? Many of the readers will be people who own Victorians and who will be delighted to find good, workable remodeling suggestions. Oh, yes, Sara, we absolutely must have that section."

Sara removed the receiver from her ear and made a horrible face at it. She returned it just in time to hear Helene demand, "Have you set up an appointment with Brady?"

"Not yet," she admitted crossly.

Helene's silence spoke volumes about the younger set and their procrastinating ways.

Wondering why she was doomed to be putty in the hands of elderly people, Sara mentally threw up her hands in surrender. "All right, Helene," she sighed, "I'll call him."

"Good." Without a pause, she directed, "Bring me the material that you've finished. Right away. When you talk to Brady, explain that this is urgent and he must drop everything to work with you."

Sara cradled the receiver. Sure, Helene. I'll just tell him to boot his models out the door and trot right over here. And he'll do precisely that. Sure he will. Staring at the telephone, she wondered what she'd really say if and when she worked up the courage to dial his number. Or, more to the point, what *he'd* say. Probably something provoking about commitments and Christmas. Then she'd get mad and hang up. And they'd be right back where they began—not talking to each other.

Deciding that writing the script in advance wasn't accomplishing anything, she pulled the phone closer. With the eraser of a pencil, she poked the buttons, listened to the buzzing ring and tried to steady her breath. Maybe he isn't home, she thought hopefully. Or maybe he's so busy with legs or toes or navels that he won't leave the studio. Before she could formulate any other hopeful excuses, the ringing ended abruptly.

"What?"

"Brady?" she asked cautiously. The snarled greeting wasn't exactly what she had expected.

"Sara?"

"Uh-hmm."

"Sorry." She heard him take a deep, steadying breath. "These girls are driving me crazy, but I didn't mean to take it out on you."

"What are they doing?" she asked curiously.

"It's what they're not doing," he growled.

Smiling, she said, "I'll bite. What aren't they doing?"

"Showing up on time, for one thing. Some aren't showing up at all. When they do, they're so busy talking about their rights as career women, they forget they ever learned to smile."

"That seems awfully out of character," she said. The ones she had met considered camera angles their major career problems.

"It is." His voice was grim. "I'll find out what it's all about and take care of it. Enough of that," he added on a lighter tone. "What can I do for you?"

Only the thought of Helene Felton drove Sara on. "It doesn't sound like very good timing," she apologized ruefully, "but I'm ready to work on that chapter with you."

"My nights are yours," he said promptly.

Sara blinked. Was he sending a subtle message or just being cooperative? she wondered. Considering that he had rejected her offer of an evening, she opted for the latter. "When?"

"Tonight?"

"Fine," she said briskly. "When can you be here?" No more of the too-cozy, too-tempting ambience of his home.

"Six-thirty?"

"Fine. See you then. And, Brady, thanks."

"If you really want to thank me—"

Sara stiffened as he paused. "Yes?" she said coolly.

"Keep Zak away from that damned piano!"

Chapter Eight

"Where did you get that?"

Sara tilted her head and admired Brady's pearl-gray Stetson as he stepped from the dimly lit entry hall into the living room. His grin was a white slash against his tanned face as he raised a long finger to the brim and tilted it back on his head. It was like something out of an old Gary Cooper movie, she thought, her amber eyes gleaming with a hint of laughter. Zak followed Brady in, shooting frankly covetous glances at the hat.

"Like it?"

"Love it," she assured him, realizing that she meant every word of it. Leading him through to the dining room, she said, "You're brave, wearing it where Zak can see it."

"I thought about it," he admitted, "but I decided he'd just have to learn who the boss is around here."

Sara grinned. "And who is?"

"We'll find that out when he makes a grab for the hat." After removing it and placing it on top of a heavy, ornately carved china cabinet, he turned to examine the stacks of pictures on the table.

"I separated them by rooms," she began. Brady's attention, she noted, was divided equally between the photos and Zak, who was sidling closer to the china cupboard. "I didn't know what else to do, but that seemed like a logical place to start and—"

"Zak, get your hand off that hat!" Brady roared.

Zak jumped guiltily. His long arm, which had been snaking up the side of the cabinet, jerked to a stop. Then his fingers closed around the brim of the Stetson and, with a quick twitch, he dropped it down on his head. With a gesture that a magician would envy, he held his hands out for inspection. *See? No hat,* his expression said clearly.

"Put it back." Brady's tone was menacing.

Zak reached out, snagged an apple from a dish on the sideboard and offered it to Brady. The hat slid down, settling on his pronounced brows. When Brady made no move to accept the apple, he stuffed it in his mouth. Using his knuckles as crutches, he turned and started out the door.

"Zak, put it back. *Now.*" Brady's crackling order stopped the ape in his tracks.

Zak looked over his shoulder, peering at Brady from beneath the brim of the hat. With his lips pursed, he looked like an old man who was either sulking or about to spit.

They eyed each other steadily, neither one blinking. Brady slowly raised his hand and pointed to the top of the cabinet. He snapped his fingers, mutely reinforcing the command.

Zak turned and, with a swagger reminiscent of a shoot-out scene in a bad western, stepped toward the cabinet. With every muscle in his body, he proclaimed that this whole thing was his idea; he wasn't under duress. He removed the hat and slowly spun it on one long finger. As it picked up speed, it sailed up and settled gently atop the cabinet. After that bit of one-upsmanship, he turned, directed a cross-eyed glare at Brady and, extending his tongue through his lips, produced a disgusting Bronx cheer. Then, knuckles to the floor, he swung through the door.

Sara breathed a gusty sigh of relief. Looking up at Brady, she asked, "What would you have done if he'd decided to run?"

He grinned wryly, slanting her a quick glance. "Beats the hell out of me. Maybe I'd have tried one of his tricks."

"Like looking cross-eyed?"

"Nothing that passive," he objected. "More along the lines of pounding the wall and throwing something at him."

"Maybe you should just have put the hat up higher."

"On what?" he asked, looking around. "I suppose I could have nailed it to the ceiling. He could reach almost anything else." He eyed her questioningly. "What's his arm span?"

A rueful smile curved Sara's lips. "About seven feet."

"That's what I thought." He shook his head. "No, my only chance was to intimidate him. Otherwise, I'd have to wear it all the time or chain it to my wrist. I don't intend to do either. Now it's settled."

Sara's heavy russet brows rose. Maybe. But she doubted it. Billy could tell him something about Zak's patience when it came to stalking hats. She began to issue a warning, but observing that his preoccupied gaze had settled on the pictures, she shrugged and joined him at the table.

Brady knew what he was doing, Sara noted thoughtfully. After running full tilt into the marauding male, it was interesting to meet his business persona. No, it was more than that—fascinating and impressive. Any woman who had the slightest interest in a man should observe him at work, she decided. It was quite a revelation.

Brady was knowledgeable and efficient, and had obviously worked on manuscripts before. He unhesitatingly selected the best pictures and succinctly explained why he chose them. He swept the rest into a pile and put them on the sideboard. Returning to the table, he leaned over Sara, one hand planted on the table beside her elbow, and organized the remaining pictures.

"I took these from the same angles so I'd get the best before-and-after effect," he said. Sara nodded, her attention shifting to the warm thumb absently stroking her arm.

"I see," she murmured, moving fractionally.

He tapped one picture of the kitchen. "See how this shows the old utility room before the wall came down?'' His large hand unconsciously closed over her arm, holding it still.

''Uh-hmm,'' she said vaguely.

Zak came in and headed for the large basket of fruit on the sideboard. Holding one arm against his body like a sling, he tucked an assortment of apples, pears and bananas along every available inch. Stuffing an apple in his mouth and two in each hand, he turned to leave.

Brady watched in wide-eyed interest. ''I'd hate to see your fruit bill for a week.''

''That bit of the national debt is Tabitha's, thank God. The supermarket produce people love her,'' Sara said, leaning back and managing to move her arm without being too obvious about it.

Turning back to the job at hand, Brady stared down at the pictures. Sara was about to follow his lead when she noticed that Zak had halted by the cabinet. He looked over his shoulder at Brady, then shot a distinctly possessive glance up at the gray hat. Satisfied that it was still there, he shambled out.

Two hours later, Brady looked at Sara. His gaze didn't have far to travel; he was sitting right next to her, his fingers laced through hers. ''I think that about wraps it up. All you have to do is add a few lines of text by each set of pictures. You can probably have it sealed and delivered in a couple of days. Then you'll have Aunt Helene out of your hair.''

Sara's relieved smile was so brilliant he blinked. ''You're a wonder,'' she said, reaching out to touch his arm. ''I would have fussed over this stuff for a couple of weeks and still been dissatisfied. I owe you one. A big one."

"I'll collect right now," he said promptly, reaching out to cover her hand with his. "I'll take you."

Sara tugged and retrieved her hand. Her resolution, she found, had a direct bearing to her proximity to him. Standing up and moving toward the door, she said matter-of-factly, "Will you settle for a piece of Mrs. Mallory's chocolate-cream pie? I think that's safer. I haven't added any more to my original offer. You do remember it, don't you? The one you found so inadequate?"

He stared at her enigmatically for a moment before he rose to stand beside her. "I remember," he said slowly. "It's not something I'll easily forget." His gray gaze held a distinct challenge.

"Pie," she said hurriedly. "I'll get it."

Before she could move, his long fingers settled beneath her chin and gently lifted her face to his. He bent his head, brushing his lips across hers in a breathless, utterly sensual movement. "I'll wait for you."

Sara gazed up at him, too startled to move. The soft words were a promise. Or a threat. It all depended upon one's point of view.

"No pie?" she asked breathlessly.

He shook his head. "No pie."

He turned and reached for his hat. Pulling it low on his forehead he said, "See me to the door?"

Sara nodded and turned away, relieved beyond measure when Zak shuffled up to join them. He snagged a banana from a fruit basket and slipped it into Brady's pocket.

Sara smiled faintly. "That's so you won't get hungry on the way home."

He leaned against the door and looked down at her. "What I'm hungry for can't be satisfied so easily," he said with stark simplicity.

Zak reached up and patted him on the shoulder.

Brady glanced down with a whimsical smile. "Thanks for the sympathy."

Zak curled his lips back in a grin while his hand inched up and he deftly rubbed the brim of the expensive gray hat between two long fingers.

"Who was that, Emily?" Sara closed the front door behind her, shrugged out of her coat and hung it in the closet.

"Who was who?" Emily said vaguely.

"The person who was driving the car I just passed. I saw you waving goodbye as I turned up the drive."

"Oh, that person." Emily smoothed back several strands of unevenly colored brown hair and secured them in a loose knot at the back of her neck. Walking over to a gilt-edged mirror, she fussed over the casual arrangement for several moments.

Sara eyed her friend's rounded reflection with concern. "Are you feeling all right, Emily?" Now that she thought about it, the older woman had seemed different lately. She couldn't put her finger on it, but Emily had had a certain air of abstraction that was out of character. Then, just as quickly as it had formed, Sara's sudden tension eased as Emily met her gaze in the mirror and smiled.

"I'm fine. Why, do I look like I'm coming down with something?" She rubbed her cheeks and examined her face with narrowed eyes. "Maybe it's my hair. I don't think this new color is exactly what I was aiming for. It looks like a variegated skein of yarn."

Sara agreed but she wasn't about to admit it. She was searching for some honest but kind words when Emily turned to her with an exasperated sound.

"That woman called again. I promised I'd tell you as soon as you came home. Of course, at that point I'd have promised anything, just to get her off the line. How you can stand that old biddy is beyond me."

"What woman?" Sara asked with a sinking feeling.

"The little one who makes all the noise."

"Mrs. Felton?" She groaned when Emily gave a grim nod. "What can she want now? I delivered the manuscript to her two days ago. She went over it with a fine-tooth comb and said it was acceptable."

"Acceptable?" Emily snorted.

"For her, that was high praise," Sara explained.

"Well, you'd better call her back before she starts burning up the wires again. I've got more important things to do than take orders from her."

Sara groaned and reached for the telephone. Helene answered on the second ring.

"Sara, where have you been? The Fancy Fair is just around the corner and I'm counting on you to help me."

"The what?" Sara asked in bewilderment. She was getting accustomed to the feeling, she decided grimly.

Every time she talked to this woman, she felt like Alice being thrust into Wonderland.

"Fancy Fair," Helene enunciated clearly, as if dealing with one who only spoke a foreign language.

"What's that?" Sara asked blankly, searching her memory for previous references to the occasion and coming up with a blank.

Helene sighed. When she spoke, exasperation fairly crackled along the line. "It's the fair we have in conjunction with the annual Holiday Home Tour. We sell homemade gifts of the Victorian era and the money helps provide financial support for our association during the year. Now, we must find the most appropriate task for you. Can you crochet?"

"No," Sara said definitely.

"Knit?"

"No."

"Cross-stitch?"

"No."

"Embroider?"

"No." Smiling in relief, Sara thought she just might make it through this occasion unscathed.

"Quilt?"

"No." She fairly sang out the word.

"Smock?"

"Absolutely not." There was a distinct pause at the other end, then Sara heard a few mumbled words. "Hopeless," was the only one she could understand. Grinning, she waited to be let off the hook.

"Well, it will have to be the wonder balls and pomanders," Helen stated flatly.

Her grin fading, Sara asked cautiously, "What's a wonder ball?"

"An item that requires absolutely no talent to make," Helene replied.

"What does it do?"

"Nothing." Apparently realizing that she had given less than a satisfactory answer, she added, "It's a very popular item with older ladies who knit or crochet."

"Exactly what does the person who is making the wonder ball do?" Sara asked carefully, refusing to associate herself with the project.

Helene had no such scruples. "You unravel a skein of yarn and rewind it with little gifts hidden inside."

Sara waited. "That's it?" she finally asked.

"Then," Helene went on, "throughout the year, as the ladies use the yarn, they uncover the gifts."

"And you say this is a big item?" Sara asked in disbelief.

"Enormously popular," Helene assured her. "You can't imagine how many we sell. And the pomanders, of course."

Sara groaned.

"You *do* know how to make pomanders?"

"Yes," Sara admitted hollowly. Didn't she still have nightmares resulting from her one and only experience preparing them? It had sounded deceptively simple. As far as that went, it still did. You took large oranges or apples and studded them with whole cloves. It was just that it took about a zillion cloves for each piece of fruit, to insure that not one microspeck of the peel was visible. Then, for days or weeks afterward, you had to babysit the suckers, turning them and sprinkling them with cinnamon and orris root.

"Good!" Helene barely concealed her amazement. "Now, what you should do first is see Ethel Brixley at the Yarn Shoppe. She ordered all the supplies—at cost, of course—and is waiting for someone to pick them up."

Sara visualized mountains of yarn, boxes of little gifts, and cans of cloves being hauled out of the yarn shop and being deposited in her car.

"Helene, I don't—"

"And the produce man said he would set aside the fruit as soon as we call."

"Helene, I—"

"Mrs. Brixley said she would explain each step of the process."

"*Helene*," Sara got out through clenched teeth, "I—"

"I'll call them now and tell them you're coming. We can discuss the home-tour details later. Oh, and Sara, perhaps you should borrow Tabitha's pickup when you go over to see Mrs. Brixley."

Sara groaned.

Sara looked up from a half-completed pomander and scowled at the ringing telephone. She jabbed another clove in the orange and decided to ignore the strident sound. It was probably just Helene with more directives, she rationalized. After ten more rings, she slammed the orange on the table and reached for the telephone.

"Hello," she snapped. If it *was* Helene, she would just tell her— "Sara? Can you come over to my place? Right now?"

The tone of Brady's voice brought her head up. She had heard him in a variety of moods, but right now he sounded as if he were struggling with several emotions—none of them pleasant.

"What's the matter?" she asked, puzzled.

"If I told you, you wouldn't believe it. *I* don't believe it, and I'm looking out the window at it!"

"Brady, I'm not really in the mood for games. I've got half an orange that I have to finish and—"

"Eat the damned thing later," he told her tightly. "Or throw it away."

The man was crazy, she decided calmly—or he had never spent an afternoon jabbing cloves in oranges. One just didn't stop halfway without facing imminent spoilage and a lot of wasted effort.

"Look," she said soothingly, "just give me an hour and I'll be over. Surely, whatever it is can wait that long." There was a silence like the lull before a storm, then she heard him take a deep, steadying breath.

"It may be able to," he told her tersely, "but I can't."

"Will you at least tell me what's going on?" she asked with a touch of asperity.

"Well, for starters, there's a crowd of women standing in front of my house with picket signs."

"What?"

"They're marching back and forth chanting something about sexist men who exploit women."

Sara closed her eyes and groaned. *Emily.* It had all the earmarks of one of her organized protests. Wondering where the state of Nevada stood on justifiable homicide, she asked weakly, "Anything else?"

"Not much."

Maybe she was wrong, Sara thought, taking a deep breath of relief. Then Brady continued in a particularly nasty tone.

"Just Emily Pinfeather, sporting red sneakers and a matching bullhorn."

"Oh, hell."

"My words exactly. Are you coming?"

"Of course, but I honestly don't know what good I'll do. When Emily rides a cause, she doesn't listen to anyone."

"Then you'd better start praying, because Emily or no Emily, I'll call the cops and have them hauled away."

"Give me ten minutes."

At that particular moment, if Sara had been asked her opinion on miracles or instant answers to prayers, her answer would have been decidedly shaky. Five minutes later, however, she was transformed into an instant believer. She had stuffed Zak in the car and was barreling down the road to Brady's when the miracle occurred. Zak extended a long arm and poked the radio buttons until he got the news. Sara had never understood his fascination with the fast-paced litany of catastrophies, but had long since stopped questioning the matter. She ignored the newscaster who muttered of the day's disasters until he mentioned California and a familiar name caught her attention.

There was no need to turn up the volume. Zak liked his daily dose of calamities served up in earsplitting decibels.

"That's it!" Sara told Zak. "That's *it*!" Diverting Emily had seemed an impossible task—until now.

Her exultant laughter faded as she pulled up in front of Brady's house. She heard Emily's voice booming through the bullhorn long before she spotted her. Women holding up signs were marching in a ragged circle, chanting along with her.

Sara's eyes widened as she read the parade of placards.

Fat Cat Photographer

Sexist

Unleash the Fetters of Fashion

Break Brady

Crush Cameron

And Emily was thundering, "Hell no, we won't go!" It was catchy, Sara admitted, but she didn't exactly see how it applied to the situation at hand.

Sara had never had the privilege of witnessing one of Emily's productions. She was impressed. If Emily could do this in an area where the trees outnumbered the population by a thousand to one, what must she be capable of in a metropolis? she wondered in awe. Reminding herself that this was not the time to be lost in admiration, she looked out the car window at some of Brady's highest-paid models.

Zak was observing the organized confusion with fascination and she had to tap him on the shoulder several times to get his attention.

"Zak," she said, signing as well as using her voice, "those are all your friends. Go show them how much you love them." Zak pursed his lips and made a loud kissing sound. Sara grinned and encouraged him. "That's right," she repeated in a quivering voice, "go love them."

The passenger door opened and Zak slid to the ground. Sara watched as he singled out a leggy blonde who was straggling behind the others. He shuffled behind her until she slowed down, then stretched up and kissed her on the cheek. She turned with a questioning look that became one of utter horror. Her shriek easily drowned out Emily's encouraging calls. Her sign shot up in the air and she stretched her long legs in a sprint for Brady's front door.

Zak approached his next target, a spectacular brunette, with shuffling gait and smacking lips. She maintained her position for several courageous moments before following the blonde. Before Zak could zero in on his next quarry, the line broke. Signs flew in all directions; legs, toes, navels and breasts made a beeline for Brady's open door.

Sara made her way through the surging crowd, feeling like a salmon going upstream. At one point, she was jabbed by a sign. Looking around, she gasped, "Ethel Brixley, what are you doing here?"

"I'm not really sure," the pleasant-faced woman told her. "Emily invited me. No, what she actually said was that it was my duty to come."

"Duty to what, or whom?" Sara asked, bewildered.

"Womanhood. At least I think that's what she said."

The two women looked at each other, then broke into identical grins.

"Emily does have a way with words, doesn't she?" Sara asked on a gurgle of laughter.

"She does indeed." Ethel drew a satisfied breath and said placidly, "I wouldn't have missed this for the world."

Sara looked around at the debacle. Zak stared longingly after the flashing legs and wiggling derrieres. He blew them a couple of kisses, then settled for picking up picket signs. Emily, in a heroic pose, brayed into the bullhorn, commanding her troops to return to their posts.

Sara excused herself and walked over to Emily.

"Come out of the house," Emily called, almost deafening Sara. "Come back and fight for your rights."

"Emily," Sara said dramatically, falling into the spirit of the moment, "there's not a moment to waste."

"Come out of there!" Emily blared.

"Your people in California, the Save the Whale group, are in trouble."

"Come out—" Emily whirled, bullhorn still held to her lips, and faced Sara. "What did you say?" she trumpeted.

Sara closed her eyes and waited for the ringing to leave her ears. She reached over to detach Emily from the bullhorn and yelled, "The Save the Whale people need you."

"No need to shout, Sara," Emily said calmly, brushing dust off her skirt. "What's the problem? Last time I checked in with them, they were just fine."

"I just heard on the news that some oil company is trying to get permission to do some offshore drilling right in the gray whales' migration path. Your group is gearing up to fight them."

Emily's stiffening frame reminded Sara of a warhorse listening to the call of a distant bugle. "They'll drill over my dead body," she said militantly. "I'll need your car, Sara. I have to pack."

Sara handed over the car keys. "Brady will take me home," she assured the older woman. She could have saved her breath, she decided. Emily hadn't reached the car yet, but she was already miles away.

Emily wasn't the only one leaving. The models were peering out of Brady's door, nervously checking Zak's whereabouts and dashing for their cars. Ethel Brixley joined the general exodus.

When the dust had settled, Sara and Zak joined Brady. He was standing on the porch, watching the last of the cars trail down the drive.

"Well, what do you think?" she asked, glancing uncertainly at his expressionless face.

He reached out and, with great precision, fit her against his taut frame. Once he had done that to his satisfaction, he held her in place by wrapping his arms around her. Then he said, "What do I think? Hell, woman, I think you're better than a platoon of marines. And," he added grimly, "I think there's about twenty top-notch models who will be slinging hash when I get through with them."

"Oh, no." Sara looked up earnestly. "Brady, it really isn't their fault. You've never heard Emily when she gets on her soapbox. She's like something out of a revival meeting. She mesmerizes people. This is the first time I've seen her in action, but I've heard about her exploits. She makes perfectly reasonable people do the most extraordinary things."

In her desire to convince him, she linked her hands behind his neck and tugged. As his eyes met hers, she said, "I mean it, Brady. Those girls really aren't responsible. And after today, they'll probably be falling all over themselves to meet your schedule. Tomorrow they'll be a changed bunch of women, you'll see."

Brady looked down at Sara's soft lips and decided he didn't care one way or another about those idiot girls. All he wanted to do was stop Sara's lips with his own, to feel her warm breath meld with his, to taste her, to hold her against his aching body. And yes, damn it, to take her upstairs to his bed, peel off those body-hugging jeans and love her until she was warm and flushed and crying out for him.

Instead, he took a steadying breath, dropped his arm to her waist and urged her through the door. Zak was propped against the newel post staring at the hall hat rack, eyeing his Stetson with an acquisitive gleam.

"No, Zak," he firmly told the ape. "I know I owe you for today. You can raid my kitchen, but you can't have my hat."

"Maybe we should go while he still has some willpower left," Sara suggested. Yes, it was definitely time to go, she decided nervously, trying to ignore the challenge suddenly gleaming down at her from the depths of smoky eyes.

"By all means," Brady said politely. "Run while you can, Sara." His quick, wolfish smile was not meant to be reassuring. "After Christmas, you can slow down—when all your deadlines have been met."

Chapter Nine

Brady loped up the walk, gave a perfunctory knock and opened Sara's door. His eyes skimmed over her with a possessive gleam as she walked down the stairs, hand lightly resting on the gleaming banister. Her jonquil jumpsuit was like a beam of sunlight radiating out to brighten the entire room. A heady scent of spices permeated the air and he turned, glancing around curiously. "Mulled cider?" he guessed.

Sara looked down at his upraised face. His quizzically peaked brows and crooked smile gave him a deceptive air of innocence. She forcibly reminded herself that while he might be helpful, competent, charming, witty, and a host of other things, he was not innocent. He had undoubtedly known that she would spend a few sleepless nights mulling over his latest challenge. And she had done exactly that, until she'd decided she could be just as cool as he was. Now, she reminded herself, was the time to show him that she wasn't the least bit threatened by him.

"Pomanders," she said succinctly.

She held a hand out for his jacket and hung it in the closet just as Zak popped in to greet his friend. With skill a pickpocket would envy, he rested his hand on Brady's shoulder and extended a long forefinger to gently caress the brim of the Stetson. For once, he didn't join them as they turned out of the entry hall.

"Coming, Zak?" Sara asked.

He shook his head and slanted a wistful glance at the gray hat.

"No," Brady told him. "I think he's trying to work on my conscience," he said to Sara.

They both stopped at the parlor door. A rainbow of fluffy yarn balls cascaded over a love seat at the far end of the room and trays of clove-studded fruit covered every available flat surface.

"Have you had a work party?" he asked, hefting a pomander and examining it closely, sniffing appreciatively before replacing it.

Sara shook her head. "Everyone else is busy quilting, smocking, crocheting, knitting or embroidering."

"Can't you knit, quilt, etcetera?"

"Sure I can."

"Then why'd you get stuck with this stuff?"

"I lied."

His brows rose in mute question marks.

"I thought if I told Helene I couldn't do anything, she'd pass me by and go on to the next victim. I didn't know how devious she was, that she had these things—" Sara waved her hand around the room "—held in reserve for the totally inept."

Brady's grin had a bit of an I-could-have-told-you-so quality to it. "You've also established a pattern," he reminded her. "What'll you do about next year?"

"Sell the house," she said grimly. His deep laughter drew a reluctant smile from her. "I'm almost serious," she assured him. "Your aunt is driving me nuts!"

"She has that effect on people," he assured her, the smile still deep in his eyes.

Sara turned away from him, wishing he wouldn't look at her like that. Without saying a word, he was reaching out, drawing her to him, making promises that she had learned years ago to mistrust, asking for emotions she had lost at the same time. "Have you talked to Helene lately?" she asked.

"Nope. I turned on the answering machine and I don't return her calls. It drives her crazy."

"Good. The only problem with that is, I get your calls *and* mine. I now have a notebook full of things to tell you."

He looked around at the gift-laden room. "I knew she'd figure something out. Is there any place to sit down while we talk?"

"In there." Sara gestured to the living room. Brady followed her, coming to an abrupt halt at a mountain of greenery piled against the wall.

"What the hell is that?"

Sara eyed him suspiciously. "Have you or have you not ever taken part in the Holiday Home Tours?"

"Not," he told her promptly.

Her expression turned to one of outright surprise. "You haven't? Why not?"

Brady shrugged carelessly. "The year after my wife died, I inherited the house from an uncle. He's the one I used to spend my summers visiting. Since then, I've always gone back east to spend the holidays with my parents." He didn't add that after meeting her, the longstanding arrangements had been altered by one quick telephone call to his family.

"What about this year?" she asked curiously.

"They're coming out for a visit after the first of the year. What about your parents?"

"I always get a ship-to-shore call from the Bahamas." Smiling, she said, "Don't look so surprised. They're nice people, but not the best parent material in the world. They dutifully raised me, but we were all relieved when I moved to California." Touched by his look of concern, she squeezed his hand and said lightly, "Don't look so distressed. We all adjusted to the situation years ago."

How do you adjust to telephone calls instead of noisy family gatherings—civility in place of love? he wondered. At least that answered the question of her undivided loyalty and love for Billy, Tabitha, Arthur, Emily and Nicholas. And he was quite sure that her daughter, Dani, would never comment so lightly or dismissingly on Sara's qualities as a parent.

"Brady? Yoo-hoo, are you there?" Sara snapped her fingers in front of his face in an effort to shift his brooding gaze from the pile of greenery. "Come on, we've got things to talk about." She pointed to a chair by the fire. "Sit there. I'll bring us some coffee."

She came back, saying, "Black, right?" At his nod, she placed the cups on a low table beside him and sat down on the floor. Crossing her legs at the ankles, she leaned back against his chair and picked up her notebook.

"Are you ready?"

His fingers skimmed over her shining hair, light as a kiss. "I guess so."

"Okay, house decorations first. Mr. Martin will be delivering a pile of evergreens to your place in a few days."

He frowned. "Who told him to?"

"Your favorite aunt."

"Not as much as you've got, I hope."

Sara smiled. "Our houses are the same size," she pointed out.

Brady's next comment was succinct and forceful.

Sara laughed outright as she pulled out a large book on Victorian Christmas decorations. "I used to think that the Victorian age was one of leisure and grace. I've changed my mind. The women obviously saved their strength to go all out for Christmas. Look at these pictures." She propped the book on his bent knees and turned to look at it with him.

Brady flipped through the pages in increasing horror. The rooms bristled with garlands and wreaths. Ropes of evergreen were wrapped over sconces, around posts and looped on stairways. They crisscrossed the ceilings and cascaded down the light fixtures. They were draped over picture frames and wrapped around wires as if they were holding up the pictures. "Kissing balls" of greens and mistletoe hung in doorways and from light fixtures. A large holly centerpiece graced the elaborately set dining-room table.

He looked up, appalled. "Who does all this?" he asked. His expression grew grim at the sight of her smile.

"Three guesses," she said dryly. "Did you think the elves came in at night and did it for you?" His reaction was almost as strong as hers, she reflected. She'd had no idea there was so much work involved in reviving authentic traditions. "But before you call Helene and tell her to take her evergreens and...make wreaths, listen to my plan."

Brady leaned back and took comfort from her vivid face. She fairly shimmered with energy. "Got a miracle up your sleeve, have you?"

"Not quite." Sara turned to face him, resting her bent elbow on his knee. "Just a division of labor. I suggest that we join forces. Helene has drawn up a schedule for the ten houses open for the tour; mine is first and yours is last."

"Is that good?"

"It couldn't be better," she replied with an emphatic nod. "This way, you can help me decorate and be my host for the evening."

"Host?"

"No wonder Helene turned you over to me," she said dryly at his blank expression. "We're acting as if these people are our guests. We greet them at the door, take them through the house—just the main floor—and explain what sort of activities took place in each room. Then we leave them in back, in the solarium, where they'll be served hot spiced punch and shortbread cookies. We come back, greet another group and start all over again."

"How many times do we do this?" he asked uneasily.

"Four. On the hour, beginning at six."

"My God," he said. "It sounds awful. How long is this going on?"

Laughing at his appalled expression, Sara said, "Ten nights. And in case you've forgotten, the curtain goes up four nights from now. And in exactly fourteen, the whole shebang will end at your house."

Brady shifted in the chair, enjoying Sara's warmth along his leg. "So far, we've taken care of your house. What about mine?"

"You keep interrupting," she said, looking up in mild complaint. "I was getting around to it. Once my house is done, then we trot over to yours and start working there. And on the seventeenth, if you want me to be your hostess, I will."

"The seventeenth?"

Sara nodded. "The night you host the tour," she repeated patiently. What was the matter with the man, she wondered, analyzing his peculiar expression. Had she placed him in an awkward position by offering to be his hostess? Well, he could always say no. But maybe she should offer him a graceful way out, just in case.

Brady shifted again, this time hardly feeling the brush of Sara's soft breast against his leg. The seventeenth. The night Nicholas had chosen for his planned escapade. Because of the new moon. When he had asked what that had to do with setting the day, the older man had shaken his head and sighed. The new moon, he'd explained patiently, meant no moonlight—therefore, no shadows. A perfect time to drop in on someone.

It was going to be a busy evening, Brady thought, staring abstractedly at the fire. Devotees of the Victorian era would be trooping through one house while, just a mile away, an accomplished cat-burglar would be checking gear and completing plans to tour another. His gaze swung back, focusing on Sara's restless hands, and realized that she was still talking.

"Of course," Sara said casually, "I don't have to do *that* part. If you just need help with the decorations, I understand. I didn't mean to make it sound like a package deal. It's not that at all. You just seemed so... overwhelmed by the whole thing—but maybe I misunderstood. All you have to do," she said, sounding a bit desperate, "is tell me what you want."

A slow, wicked grin relaxed his face. Sara, his sweet, composed Sara, was dithering. And delightfully, too.

"I know," she plowed on valiantly, "that there are any number of women you could ask—"

"Honey," he mercifully interrupted, "what the hell are you talking about?"

She glared up at his smiling face, thoroughly annoyed. "I'm trying," she said with a snap, "to let you off the hook. Gracefully."

"What hook?"

Irritably blowing a strand of hair out of her eyes, she muttered, "About my being your hostess for the evening."

Brady might have restrained himself if she had maintained her usual cool control, but he was irresistibly drawn to her expression of harassed embarrassment. He leaned over, scooped her up in his arms and dropped her in his lap. "I don't want off the hook, gracefully or any other way. I want you, whenever and however I can get you."

"Well, why didn't you say so?" she questioned with a belligerent scowl. "You let me—"

His lips stopped her. This time there was no soft tasting, no persuasive brushing. His kisses—pulse-pounding, blood-thundering kisses—asked for, demanded, if not surrender, at least a total sharing. He wanted her to acknowledge her own hunger, to claim what she wanted. The soft sigh of his name and the gentle kneading fingers on his nape betrayed her, but when he lifted his head her eyes remained stubbornly closed. He bent to drop one last kiss on her silky, love-swollen lips.

"Okay, love," he sighed. "Time for me to get going." He eased her to her feet and watched as she draped composure around her like a cloak.

"I'll get your coat," she said breathlessly, and turned away.

Brady slowly followed, never taking his eyes off her, even as he reached for his jacket.

Her flustered eyes followed his arms as they slid into the sleeves.

"Funny," he muttered. "I thought I left my keys in the pocket."

They both looked down at the floor. Sara opened the closet and checked that floor.

"It's okay," Brady told her. "Maybe I left them in the ignition."

"And if you didn't?"

"I have another set hidden in the car." He bent his head for one last, slow, sweet kiss. "Night, love," he murmured, then walked out the door.

Sara watched the car lights spring on, then slide down the drive as she stood at the open door and dreamed long-forgotten dreams. Finally driven inside by the cold, she was startled by the mirrored reflection of her flushed, wistful expression. "Don't even think about it, Sara," she warned herself firmly, watching the softened look fade. "Don't be crazy. It won't work."

"You're crazy, Nick. It won't work!" Brady said for the second time, glowering at the madman who temporarily occupied his friend's body. If Nicholas's expression was any indication, he was merely waiting for the verbal storm to recede before continuing to outline his plan.

"I thought you just needed a little more time to think the idea through," Brady said, running an agitated hand through his hair. "But, no, you're still as determined as ever!"

Nicholas nodded placidly. "Quite."

Brady tightened the belt of his velvet robe and took a turn around the room in his bare feet. "Let me see if I have this straight," he said, not bothering to conceal his sarcasm. "You decided that you'd better practice your rappeling, right?"

Nicholas nodded again, a glint of humor in his hooded eyes.

"And you woke me up at one in the morning to go with you, right?"

Nicholas smiled an affirmative.

"On a blustery December night," he finished in disbelief, "you want me to freeze my butt off somewhere in the mountains sliding down ropes." It was now a statement.

"That's right."

"Nick, despite all your planning, I think you forgot one small detail."

"What's that?" Nicholas looked up, more with curious interest than alarm.

"I take it the overhang is well away from the side of the mountain?"

The older man nodded for a third time.

"Then how are you going to get back up? No one could climb back up that rope, even with the encouragement of snarling Dobermans. Or do you have a winch up there with some fancy remote-control starter?"

Nicholas winced with distaste. "I'm not James Bond," he stated. Then, smiling at Brady's "gotcha" expression, he slowly extended his hand. "Remember these?" he asked.

Taken off guard by the casual question, Brady stepped forward and looked at the item in Nick's hand. A spasm crossed his face. Any well-trained climber knew damned well what they were. They looked like brass knuckles, but they were ascending devices for climbing ropes. They weren't fast, but they were effective.

"It'll take forever," he stated bluntly.

Nicholas sighed. It irked him to admit that on this particular point, Brady was correct. "It's the one weak spot in my plan," he admitted. "And I've gotten a bit rusty. That's why I'm going out tonight—and every other night until the seventeenth, if necessary." He stood and looked consideringly at Brady. "Coming with me?"

The last thing in the world Brady wanted to do was go out into the cold dark night and practice rappelling. It might have been tolerable during the day but Nicholas, a stickler for details, insisted on the dark. The real project, he stated, was at night; ergo, all run-throughs would also be at night. But it was one thing to want to go back to his warm bed, another to actually do it—especially when he could visualize the pain that would rack Sara if anything happened to Nicholas. Add to that the fact that he could no more let an old man tackle such a venture alone than he could picture himself accompanying Nicholas on the seventeenth, and what did you have? A sucker, he told himself.

"Let me get my clothes," Brady said.

"What do you think?" Sara revolved slowly in front of Tabitha and waited for her opinion. The older woman often dressed like a refugee, but she had a keen sense of style where others were concerned. The two women were in Sara's cream and apricot bedroom.

Tabitha eyed her approvingly. The outfit Sara had chosen to wear for the home tour was a long, garnet velvet skirt and a white lace blouse. The skirt fit snugly at the waist and the blouse had long, flowing pirate-like sleeves buttoned at the wrist and a low, square-cut neckline. Pearl earrings and a slender gold chain with a pearl teardrop added the finishing touches.

"I think you would have set the Victorian era on its ear. The men would have made illicit offers and the women would've tried to run you out of town."

"Hmm." Sara turned back to the mirror and stared dubiously at her reflection. She touched the neckline, tracing the straight line just above her breasts. "Do you think it's too...?"

"No." There was a wide range of meaning in the negative answer.

"No?"

Tabitha heaved a sigh. "No. No, it's not too low; no, the people won't be shocked; no, Brady won't think you're a walking advertisement; and no, don't touch it."

"All that in one simple word?" Sara smiled, but her eyes still doubted.

"All that and whatever else you need," Tabitha said in exasperation. "Is everything done downstairs?"

"Yes. I think so. I hope so."

The past few days had been busy ones and, to Sara's surprise, enormously enjoyable. She wired together long ropes of evergreens, made wreaths for the windows and fireplaces, and kissing balls to hang in doorways and from light fixtures. As a final touch, she added quantities of red bows and ribbons. Brady spent each evening on a ladder hanging the streamerlike greens. Zak was a fascinated observer, supporting the ropes so they wouldn't tangle and occasionally trying to eat the pomanders.

Now the work was all done. Helene was downstairs with a traveling crew that would move to a different house each night: someone to open the door, one to play the piano in the parlor, one dressed in a maid's uniform to stand by the elaborately set dining-room table, and several to serve refreshments and sell the gift items in the solarium. Helene, of course, handled the money.

"What are you going to do tonight?" Sara asked. Her friends had each dealt with the confusion in their own way. Arthur had hibernated with his computer; Emily, of course, was gone, saving the whales; Billy had chased down a rodeo in California; Nicholas was preoccupied, spending more time than usual in his suite; and Tabitha had devoted the last few days to keeping Zak out of trouble.

"I think I'll take Zak out to his room and give him a good workout on the trampoline, then keep him in my rooms. I don't think the tourists are ready for a pocket-picking orangutan."

Sara turned, eyebrows raised. "When did he start that?"

"Just a little something he's learning for his new film. He's already got a wastebasket full of stuff he's collected around here. If you're missing anything, check with him." Tabitha hesitated, then said, "Sara, you know I don't have an ounce of tact in my whole body, don't you?"

"Yes." Indeed she did. Tabitha said exactly what was on her mind, usually at the moment it occurred to her. And usually her timing was rotten.

"All I want to know is, when are you going to put Brady out of his misery? And don't say 'What misery?' You know exactly what I'm talking about. The man's crazy about you."

"Tabitha, we've only known each other a little over three months. You don't make serious decisions without serious thought."

"*You* don't. Any other woman would have snapped him up two months ago. For heaven's sake, Sara, what do you want? When you two are together, you generate enough electricity to light up this whole house!"

"I know," she said starkly, "and it scares the devil out of me."

"What's the matter with him?" Tabitha asked more quietly.

Sara's smile was a miserable failure. "Nothing—aside from the fact that he ties me up in knots."

Tabitha waved a careless hand. "Oh, that." Looking at her watch, she said, "Speaking of the devil, he should be here any minute."

"Oh, Lord, I'm going to be late," Sara groaned. "Would you go down and wait for him? I have to fix my hair."

"You just finished doing it," Tabitha reminded her dryly.

"Oh. Well, I need some perfume or something. What I really need," she said, drawing a deep breath, "is a minute to relax." Glancing at the other woman, she said, "Can you tell I'm nervous?"

"Yes," Tabitha said with her usual bluntness, opening the bedroom door. "Take a few deep breaths. Just make sure you don't hyperventilate."

Sara breathed a small sigh of relief. Her nerves really were a bit jagged and her old friend's storm-trooper tactics hadn't helped. She reached for her cologne and dabbed the light floral scent on her wrists, behind her ears and in the small shadowy hollow between her breasts. It wasn't so much the tourists, she decided. Brady had been different these past few days. *Preoccupied* would be the best word to describe it, she decided. He hadn't once mentioned deadlines or Christmas, and that in itself was enough to set her teeth on edge.

And she was no nearer a decision than she had been three months ago. She— "Sara," Tabitha called. "Brady's here."

Taking a last unnecessary swipe at her hair, she opened the door and plastered a smile on her face. It faded as soon as she walked to the landing and looked down at Brady. He looked every bit the elegantly dressed landowner, from his dark, gray-flecked hair to his gleaming leather shoes. His dark-blue suit fit to perfection. His crisp white shirt made his tan look even darker and his tie almost matched the color of her skirt.

But it was the expression on his face that stopped Sara dead in the middle of the stairs. It was a combination of hunger, urgency and pure male possessiveness. It backed up the breath in her lungs, leaving her a bit light-headed. As he climbed the stairs, his gaze met and held hers. Stopping two steps below her, he said huskily, "My God, you're beautiful. The last thing I want is to have a bunch of people pouring through that door, looking at you."

Looking at *my* woman. Sara heard the words as clearly as if he had shouted them. She had almost regained her breath when he added, "I won't ruin your makeup, but if I'm going to survive the night, I've got to do this." She was prepared for the light touch of his lips on hers. What she didn't expect was for Brady to dip his head and brush his mouth just slightly above the square neckline of the blouse.

Sucking in her breath as his mustache skimmed her tender flesh, Sara raised her hands to his shoulders, steadying herself. His hair was still slightly damp from the shower, and her nose twitched as she inhaled the wonderful essence of spicy after-shave and his personal, clean scent.

The sound of a throat being cleared shifted Sara's attention. She looked down and noticed for the first time the woman Helene had stationed at the door.

"I think the first group is coming," she hissed.

Brady stepped aside and offered Sara his arm. Feeling very much like a Victorian lady, she slipped her arm in his and walked down beside him. As they neared the bottom, the door opened and about thirty people poured in.

It wasn't as difficult as she'd thought it would be, Sara reflected after a few moments. At the last minute, she'd decided that since the original house had no electricity, she would use the lighting common to that period. She and Brady led the people into rooms cheerfully brightened with candlelight and oil lamps, discussing the typical family Christmas traditions.

When they reached the parlor, Sara invited the visitors to be seated while Milly Lee, Helene's assistant, played the piano. As soon as the foot-shuffling had ceased, Milly swung into action. After several rollicking numbers, she segued into a waltz. Sara watched, puzzled, as Brady moved to the center of the room and, with the toe of one shoe, slid one of the area rugs aside. Returning, he stopped before her and extended his hand.

With his eyes smiling warmly into hers, he said formally, "May I have the pleasure of this dance?"

Sending up a fervent prayer that waltzing was no more forgettable than bicycle riding, Sara stepped into his arms. After a moment, when she realized that she was not going to disgrace herself, she relaxed. Whirling around the polished floor, she almost managed to forget the visitors.

"There are some advantages to age." Brady spoke softly in her ear. When she looked up, he added, "Can you imagine any of the younger generation being able to do this?"

Smiling, she shook her head.

"Do you reverse, Sara Clayton?" he murmured.

Feeling as if she were answering a question that involved far more than a dance step, she admitted shakily, "On occasion, Brady Cameron."

Smoothly changing direction, Brady tightened his arm around her slim waist. "Christmas is almost here, sweetheart."

Sara stiffened.

After dropping a kiss on her gleaming hair, he said, "I'm serving notice, Sara. If you don't come to me by that time, I'm taking things into my own hands."

Speaking through clenched teeth while she tried to smile for their fascinated audience, she whispered tightly, "Are you threatening me?"

The pianist wound up with a flourish; Brady whirled Sara down the room. He raised her hand to his lips in a courtly gesture. Then his eyes locked with hers and with a grin he murmured, "You bet your sweet butt I am, lady."

Chapter Ten

Ten evenings later, Sara, once again wearing her velvet skirt and lace blouse, and Brady, in a dark suit, stood on his front porch and watched Helene's workers straggle down the walk to their cars. The last tour of the season had ended several hours before and the entire Holiday Home Tour cast had assembled at Brady's for a self-congratulatory party.

Fighting a feeling of letdown, Sara said lightly, "Well, we did it." Her words broke off as a sudden shiver shook her body. The locals had informed her that this was an unusually warm spell, but it was still considerably colder than Southern California.

Brady dropped his arm around her waist and drew her against his warm body. "You're frozen," he growled, turning her back into the house. "Why didn't you say something?"

Sara shrugged dismissingly. "I knew we wouldn't be out there long." She stopped suddenly, bringing him to a halt beside her. Looking down through the parlor into the living room, she said, "It's lovely, isn't it?"

The house smelled like a forest, and almost looked like one. Boughs of beribboned greenery gleamed in the candle-lit rooms. Ropes of it hung from every corner and trailed over every flat surface—even the clock. "My God," Sara said, astonished, "it's almost one-thirty. We've been at it since the crack of dawn. And you," she added, scrutinizing the dark face above her, "look like you haven't slept in a week."

Actually, it had been three weeks since he'd had a full night's rest, Brady reflected. And the last two, since he had decided he couldn't allow Nicholas to venture out on the new-moon flit by himself, had been especially hectic. That was when he had thrown himself heart and soul into the midnight practice sessions. And now, he had precisely thirty minutes to change into dark clothes and meet his partner in crime.

"Here," Sara said, handing him a candle snuffer. Attributing his silence to fatigue, she ordered briskly, "You start in that room, I'll work in here. As soon as we get the candles out, I'm going home so we can both get some rest."

Within minutes Brady was walking her out to her car. He turned the key in the lock, then stopped with his arm blocking the way. Swearing softly, he muttered in self-disgust, "You shouldn't be driving home alone." He cast a quick, concerned glance at his watch. "I'll take you in my car."

Misinterpreting his expression, Sara snagged her keys from his hand and slid behind the steering wheel. "Don't be silly. There's nothing between our places except one empty road and lots of trees. I'll be fine. You get some sleep."

"Sara."

She looked up, startled by his serious tone.

"Yes?"

He bent down and dropped a hard, swift kiss on her lips. "Nothing. I'll talk to you tomorrow." Brady watched until the gleam of her taillights disappeared, then turned and loped back to the house.

Actually, Sara decided as she pulled up in front of her house, she wasn't all that tired; in fact, she was still riding high on adrenaline. The tours had ended successfully and the party had been fun. Any other time, she would have enjoyed settling down with a glass of wine and hashing over the evening's events. But not tonight.

Removing the key from the ignition, she leaned back in the seat, a frown furrowing her forehead as she thought of Brady. Tonight he had acted the part of the gracious host to perfection, but that's exactly what it was—an act. His tension had been palpable, there had been no spontaneous invitation to dance, and he was undeniably tired. Yes, she decided, she had been wise to leave.

Sara brightened as she opened the front door. Good, Tabitha was still up. Calling out to see if the older woman wanted a glass of wine, Sara kicked off her shoes and padded out to the kitchen. Returning with two brimming glasses, she gave one to Tabitha and curled up in an outsize chair, her skirt a brilliant splash against the brocade material.

"Well," Tabitha demanded, "how'd it go?"

"Smoothly." Sara tasted the wine and nodded approvingly.

"And the party?"

"It was fun."

Tabitha snorted. "I've heard more enthusiasm in a dirge. What's the matter?"

"Nothing," Sara protested unconvincingly.

"Sara!"

"I'm just a little worried about Brady," she finally admitted. Spurred on by Tabitha's patent interest, she described the evening and Brady's uncharacteristic behavior.

"It's obvious what's the matter with him," said Tabitha of the one-track mind. "You're driving him crazy. I told you that ten days ago. When are you going to put that man out of his misery?" she demanded.

Sara stared at the crystal glass, a slow, secret smile curving her lips. "Tomorrow," she said simply.

"You're going to say yes?" Tabitha asked, holding her breath.

Sara nodded.

"Just like that?"

Sara's husky laugh was a soft sound in the warm room. "Yeah, after three months of agonizing, just like that. I finally realized that I didn't want to hide anymore. Brady isn't Roger. I can trust him with my life and my love," she said simply. "I want him just as much as he wants me."

"And you're waiting until tomorrow?" Tabitha asked in a scandalized tone. "Why not tonight?"

Trust Tabitha to cut to the heart of the matter, Sara thought ruefully. "It's going to be hard enough tomorrow to explain why it's taken me so long to come to my senses," she explained carefully. "I don't have the courage to pound on his door in the middle of the night and get him out of bed to tell him."

"If I know Brady, he'll probably haul you to his bed and ask for explanations in the morning," Tabitha stated.

"You think so?" Sara asked hopefully.

"I know so." After a thoughtful moment she said, "And I have something that will make it easier. At least you won't have to pound on his door. Zak apparently pinched a set of Brady's keys. At least, I assume they're his; there's a medallion on the ring with his initials. I found them the other day under that glass ball on the newel post and meant to return them. As a matter of fact," she admitted, "I'll be glad to get rid of them. I've caught Zak several times sneaking out the door with the keys. I wouldn't be surprised if he's planning to go after Brady's hat. Do you want them?"

Sara stood up, smiling in anticipation. "Yes."

Tabitha bustled from the room, grinning from ear to ear. She was back almost at once, breathing hard. "Sara! Zak's gone and so are the keys!"

Sara closed her eyes and swore. "Come on," she said, slipping into her shoes, "we've got to get him. If Brady's alarm goes off, the police will be swarming all over the place."

Tabitha pulled two coats from the closet and tossed one to Sara. "Let's take my truck."

"How much of a head start do you think he has on us?" Sara asked as they ran out the door.

"Not sure," Tabitha gasped. "But he was in my room right before you came home."

"Then maybe we have a chance."

"This isn't exactly the way I pictured you going back," Tabitha said, gunning the motor.

It wasn't precisely what she'd had in mind, either, Sara silently admitted. "Brady gave me his keys one day when he had to run into Reno," she said aloud, watching the speedometer needle climb steadily upward. "He showed me how to work the alarm panel. There's a thirty-second grace period from the time the door key is inserted in the lock and the code is punched in."

Tabitha turned the wheel and screeched into Brady's curving driveway.

"Look!" Sara pointed ahead. Zak was briefly illuminated by the bright lights as he swung up the walk to the porch. "Hurry up!"

Tabitha brought the car to a screaming stop by the walk. "Go after him, Sara. You can move faster than I can."

Sara was out and running before the other woman killed the motor. "Zak!" she commanded. "Come here!"

Her words merely spurred him on. He scrambled up the stairs and poked the key in the lock.

"Zak, damn it, come here!"

Tabitha slammed the truck door just as Zak turned the key. He pushed on the door and swung over the threshold. Sara raced up the stairs and ran across the porch, her high heels tapping on the wood. Once inside, she kicked them off and ran the few feet to the alarm. Throwing open the panel door, she quickly punched in the code. Then she sagged against the wall and held her breath. If the alarm was going to blow, she thought, it would be any second.

When nothing had happened by the time Tabitha rushed through the door, Sara knew they were home safe. Now all she had to worry about was Brady rushing down the stairs with a gun to repel the invaders.

"Where is that damn ape?" Tabitha hissed.

"Shh! For heaven's sake, keep quiet! He's probably down here." Sara groped for Tabitha's hand and led her slowly down the dark hall.

"Let's turn on a light."

"Are you crazy?"

"Just a little one," Tabitha muttered, extending her foot carefully before her.

In the time it took to creep down to the hat rack, their eyes adjusted to the lack of light. They had no trouble finding Zak. He was standing in front of a large, gilt-edged mirror, trying on the Stetson.

He slid it to the back of his head like a country boy's straw hat and squinted at the mirror. Apparently not thrilled with the image, he lifted it and plunked it straight down until he looked like an undersize Mountie in an oversize hat. Next, he slid it sideways until it jauntily covered one eye. His other eye rolled from left to right as Tabitha and Sara loomed up behind him.

"Zak," Tabitha ordered in a stern whisper, "put it back."

He grabbed the brim with both hands and tugged on the hat until it covered his eyes and a good portion of his face. Then he shook his head slowly back and forth.

Sara looked at Brady's pride and joy and knew it would never be the same. "Tabitha," she said nervously, "I think we'd better get out of here. You can tell Brady about the hat tomorrow."

"Zak!" Tabitha hissed. "I said, put it back."

Scrunching down, he wrapped his long arms over his head, somehow managing to keep his hands clamped to the brim.

"It's hopeless," Sara whispered. "Let's go."

"I can't let him get away with something like this. He'll think he can disobey me any time he wants."

Sara raised her eyes and prayed for divine intervention. When nothing happened, she muttered, "Tabitha, this isn't the time to worry about discipline. Let's *get out of here*!"

After a long stubborn silence, Tabitha gave a gusty sigh of disapproval. "All right." She reached down and touched Zak's hand. He instinctively tightened his grasp on the hat. "Come on, Zak, let's go to the truck."

He slowly relaxed his arms. Still hanging on to the brim with a strangulating grip, he raised the hat until he could peer out from beneath it. He studied Tabitha's face for a long moment. Then he loosened one hand and reached for hers.

Sara sagged in relief. She had seen these confrontations before; sometimes they lasted for hours. Before Tabitha could think better of her capitulation, she herded them down the hall.

Tabitha turned to Sara when they reached the door. "There's no reason for you to come back with us," she said. "You were on your way here already, so stay."

Why not? Sara thought, examining her friend's determined expression. Nothing had really changed. This was her chance to show Brady that she needed him. That she wanted him. After all the chasing he had done, he deserved to know that she was coming to him willingly, not simply being taken captive. A slow, wicked grin lit her face.

"Good. Although I must say," Tabitha commented dryly, walking out the door, "you'll be lucky if you can wake him up. When that man sleeps, he *sleeps*!"

Sara waited while they went down the stairs and walked to the truck. Wincing at the screech of tires, she closed the door and reset the alarm. Then, with her hand on the banister, she crept up the stairs—although it was absurd to tiptoe around at this point, she decided. Tabitha was right; Brady could sleep through an invasion.

Sara stopped at his door in sudden embarrassment, wishing she had given the matter a bit more thought. How did a modern woman, a "today's" woman, handle such a situation? she wondered. Did she go in, tap him on the shoulder and invite him to take part in a meaningful discussion regarding their relationship? Did she simply disrobe and crawl into bed with him? And if she did, did she wait to be discovered or "accidentally" scoot over and bump into him?

She leaned against the doorjamb, gloomily gnawing at her lower lip. If Tabitha hadn't cut off her retreat, she reflected, she just might have second thoughts about the whole thing. She hovered there, pondering over a universal truth: it was one thing to make a decision, entirely another to act on it.

Bracing her shoulders, she moved into the room. "Brady?" she whispered. "Brady?" Then, worried by the quality of silence in the room, she moved to the dresser and snapped on the lamp.

"Well, hell," Sara said, staring at the undisturbed, empty bed.

Brady closed the door behind him and automatically coded the alarm. Then he leaned against the wall and closed his eyes. What a night. What a *bitch* of a night. He'd be lucky if he made it up the stairs. Hell, he'd be lucky if he made it *to* the stairs. And Nicholas, the man he'd gone to protect? When they got back to the car, he looked like he'd been out for an afternoon stroll. Immaculate as ever, he'd tidily stowed away the ropes and commented that it had gone quite well, even suggested that they might team up for another venture in the near future.

Brady straightened up and groaned. Everything hurt, right down to and including his fingernails and eyelashes. If he made it up the stairs, he might live—because then he could collapse in the bathtub, turn on the jets and let them pummel his sore muscles for a while. Flipping the light switch at the bottom of the stairs, he started up—and stopped dead on the third step.

There, a few stairs up, following the curve of the staircase, splashed in brilliant contrast to the muted green rug, was Sara's velvet skirt. Barely aware of moving, he bent over to pick it up. The plush fabric carried traces of her delicate floral fragrance. Draping it over his arm, he slowly lifted his eyes.

At his next stop, he collected her white lace blouse. Above that, on the landing, was a wisp of flesh-colored lace. Outside his bedroom door, he bent down and collected a matching filmy bit of nothing. With his heart pounding as wildly as it had earlier, when he'd been dangling a hundred feet between anything solid, he nudged open the door.

Sara was in Brady's bed, wondering for the hundredth time what she was doing there and regretting her impetuous action. She was clad in his dark-blue silk pajama top, leaning back against several pillows she had pummeled into shape, trying to read a book. She had also had time to conjure up a host of real and imaginary worries. What if he had changed his mind? What if he had been out with a woman? What if, for God's sake, he came *home* with a woman? She was on the verge of trotting out and climbing back into the clothes she had so artistically displayed on the staircase when she heard Brady's deliberate footsteps approach the door. In anticipation she leaned back and closed the book.

Her breath caught as Brady stepped into the room. He wore black jeans and a black turtleneck sweater. The bright skirt and lacy feminine clothing tangled in his hands merely served to intensify his bone-deep masculinity. He was, she decided warily, more than a little intimidating.

"You look like Cary Grant in *To Catch a Thief*," she said faintly.

He winced, wishing that her comment hadn't come quite so close to the truth. As much to distract her as to settle a vital question, he lifted the clothing in his hands. "Was this a message?" he asked.

The intensity of his gaze left Sara speechless. She nodded.

"A commitment?"

Trust him to brush nonessentials aside and get to the heart of the matter, she thought wryly. He still hadn't taken his eyes off her. She nodded again.

"A *lifetime* commitment?"

What did the man want? she wondered wildly. A written contract? She nodded a third time.

He dropped the clothes on a chair as if they had become too heavy to hold. Standing by the foot of the bed, he said with a whimsical smile, "You look a lot better in that outfit than I do." Turning away, he pulled the heavy sweater over his head.

Sara's eyes widened. The mat of hair on his chest matched the thick waves on his head: dark with a sprinkling of gray. Her gaze traveled over a broad chest, muscular shoulders and a trim waist. As good as Brady looked in clothes, she thought, he improved with each layer that was peeled off.

"Sara?"

She looked up as he unzipped his jeans. Forcing her gaze away from his hands, she glanced up and became submerged in the smoky depths of his eyes.

"I love you."

Sara closed her eyes at the stark simplicity of the words, the absolute sincerity. This was a man who didn't say those words lightly, she knew. He would match her fidelity with fidelity, trust with trust, love with love.

Brady watched as her lashes grew damp and stuck together. He had never seen anyone look quite so vulnerable.

"Sara?"

She heard the smile in his voice and looked up again.

"I'm also damnably tired and sore. Will you come in and talk to me while I take a hot bath?"

Sara saw the need in his face, and the weariness. She threw back the blanket and swung her legs over the side of the bed. Brady kicked off his jeans and watched as she walked toward him. The pajama top engulfed her. In the loose garment she was primly covered and sexy as hell. He waited until she touched his extended hand with hers, then, clad only in very brief briefs, led her into the bathroom and turned on the faucets.

Sara had to raise her voice to be heard over the thunder of the water. "What have you been doing? Why were you so late?"

Brady grinned tiredly. "You sound like a wife, Sara."

"Is that bad?"

"No. As a matter of fact, I can't think of anything nicer." He unself-consciously peeled off his briefs, tossed them in a hamper and turned off the water.

Sara's eyes never left him. She watched the flex of shoulder and thigh muscles as he moved. Her gaze followed his mat of chest hair down to where it narrowed, all but disappeared, picked up again and merged with hair-roughened thighs. She devoured him with her eyes. "You are one gorgeous hunk, Brady Cameron," she said with simple honesty. Amused at the expression that crossed his face, she added on a gurgle of laughter, "And you blush!"

"I guess I do," he retorted blandly. "But I've never had an almost-naked woman look at me like she wants to wrestle me to the floor." Smoothly turning the tables, he asked politely, "Are you coming in, sweetheart?" Then he slid into the churning water and waited, eyeing her expectantly. His brows rose slowly as she hesitated.

Was this the way she was going to spend the rest of her life, she wondered ruefully, with her knees turning to water every time he looked at her? Yes, she decided, slowly undoing the buttons of the outsize top, it was. And for the life of her, she couldn't think of a better fate.

Fair is fair, she reflected, letting the fabric slip off her shoulders to the floor. She had certainly looked her fill; now it was his turn.

And look he did. Damn his silvery eyes, she fumed silently, he didn't miss a thing—not even the five freckles on her hip; or the way her body was reacting. The protracted silence drove her crazy. She couldn't tell a thing from his expression.

"What do you think?" she said in a shaky attempt at humor. "Do I need an overhaul?"

"You need nothing, sweetheart," he growled, touched by her uncertain expression. "Absolutely nothing." As she slid in beside him, he added blandly, "You blush, too," and watched with pleasure as the color flared even hotter in her cheeks.

Sara eased into the inviting curve of his arm and rested her head on his shoulder. "It's strange," she said thoughtfully.

"What is?" he asked when she left the words hanging.

"We've skipped all the preliminaries," she told him. "And yet here we are. Together."

"And that's how we'll always be," he informed her.

"We haven't even made love."

Brady groaned. "And we probably won't tonight, either," he told her bluntly, even as he ran a questing hand down her water-slick curves.

Startled, she looked up. "Why not?"

"Because I feel like I've been trampled by a herd of elephants."

Sara sat up abruptly. "Exactly what were you doing tonight?"

He tugged her back. "Being led astray by one of your sexagenarians."

She reared up again. "Nicholas! I'll murder that man!"

Brady grinned lazily, enjoying the sight of her indignation. Pulling her back against him, he murmured, "Why pick on Nicholas?"

"Because he's the only one who does midnight flits. What did you do?"

What the hell, he thought, she'd worm it out of him sooner or later. Basking in the concern radiating from her hazel eyes, Brady told her.

"Just to prove he was better than the system?" she asked.

"Uh-hmm," he agreed.

"You crawled off a mountain and slid down ropes?" To Sara, who got dizzy on the third rung of a ladder, it sounded like the act of a madman.

"That was the easy part."

Sara groaned.

"I was more concerned about the dogs."

"What dogs?" she asked ominously.

"The Dobermans."

"Oh, my God."

"Yeah," he said laconically, "that's what I said to Nicholas."

"And what did he say?"

"That they were on the ground, and we'd be on the fourth floor."

"Oh." She sighed and leaned back against him, her hand resting on his thigh.

"What he neglected to tell me was that there were stairs that connected all of the floors."

"Oh, my God."

His words, Brady remembered grimly, had been more direct. Especially since Nicholas had chosen the moment they landed to mention the fact. He had spent every second they were there in a cold sweat. Nicholas, he thought again, definitely had a warped sense of humor. "But he said that the dogs wouldn't hear us, and he was right."

Brady groaned as a jet of warm water vibrated against his shoulder. The sound deepened as Sara curled closer and wrapped her arms around his waist.

"Then what happened?" she murmured.

"It was an education to see Nick in action," he admitted. "In spite of his age, he's all whipcord muscle. And I doubt if he has a nerve in his entire body." His hand absently traced the curve of her soft bottom. "He played hell with their system." Grinning reminiscently, he said, "You should have seen him, Sara. He moved around like a shadow, busting through their precious codes and sensors as if they didn't exist. Then you know what he did?"

Sara smiled against his shoulder. If his growing enthusiasm was any indication, she was going to have her hands full keeping him away from Nicholas. But that was all right, she decided, letting him support her weight; she always had loved a challenge. "What?" she mumbled, trailing her hand down his chest.

Brady stiffened as her hand drifted lower. "He, uh, tucked his business card behind paintings, under collector's items, even inside the wall safe."

"I think Nicholas is a closet romantic," she decided, following the intriguing trail of hair down his stomach.

"And I think I've had enough." Brady surged to his feet, bringing Sara with him.

"Of what?" she asked, blinking innocent eyes. Unfortunately, her grin spoiled the effect.

Brady noted with interest that the cooler air had an immediate impact on Sara's trim body. He reached for a towel and with long, slow strokes, dried her. Handing her another towel, he said, "Your turn," and stood, waiting. His love wasn't nearly as venturesome when she wasn't concealed by churning water, he reflected, tender amusement warming his eyes.

An involuntary tightening of his body drew Sara's eyes to his. "These hot tubs are amazingly beneficial for, ah, sore muscles," she said blandly.

Brady wrapped his arms around her and she could feel the laughter vibrating in his chest. He bent his head and dropped a tender kiss on her lips. "Sara, are you really going to make an honest man of me?"

She nodded, her love written all over her face.

He tucked her to his side and led her to the big bed.

Later, Sara raised her head from his chest and looked down at him. She touched his face with gentle fingers, lovingly tracing the crease in his cheek.

"When?" he demanded.

"Tomorrow," she replied promptly.

"Where?"

"My house. Dani's coming home for the holidays, Emily is leaving the whales for a few days, and Billy's rodeo is over. Everyone will be there. And we'll invite the new pastor to dinner and ask him to perform the ceremony."

The last trace of tension left his body. He slid his hands down over her bottom and pressed her to him. Her soft body flowed over him, her legs rested on his.

Sara jerked with sudden remembrance. "Oh, Brady," she wailed, "I forgot to tell you something awful!"

Brady's stomach knotted. Damn it! He'd *known* it was too good to be true. "What?"

"You're going to be mad," she predicted gloomily.

"What, woman, *what*?"

"Zak broke into your house tonight and stole your hat."

"Damn it, Sara!"

She propped her bent elbows on his chest and looked down at him. "I knew you'd be mad."

"I'm *not* mad. You just scared the life out of me."

"You're not mad?" she asked in disbelief.

Sara's restless movement had awakened another, entirely different emotion in Brady.

"I'm not," he vowed, and with a swift movement, shifted her beneath him. "In fact," he promised, dropping a kiss on her parted lips, "we'll give it to him as a wedding present."